ERIN BEDFORD

UNTIL SUNSET

Until Sunset © 2020 Embrace the Fantasy Publishing, LLC

Also by Erin Bedford

The Underground Series
Chasing Rabbits
Chasing Cats
Chasing Princes
Chasing Shadows
Chasing Hearts
The Crimes of Alice
Hatter's Heart

The Mary Wiles Chronicles
Marked by Hell
Bound by Hell
Deceived by Hell
Tempted by Hell

Starcrossed Dragons
Riding Lightning
Grinding Frost
Swallowing Fire
Pounding Earth

The Crimson Fold
Until Midnight
Until Dawn
Until Sunset

Curse of the Fairy Tales
Rapunzel Untamed
Rapunzel Unveiled
Rapunzel Unchained

<u>**Her Angels**</u>
Heaven's Embrace
Heaven's A Beach
Heaven's Most Wanted

<u>**House of Durand**</u>
Indebted to the Vampires
Wanted by the Vampires
Protected by the Vampires
Embrace of the Vampires
Tempted by the Butler
Loved by the Vampires
Huntress of the Vampires

<u>**Academy of Witches**</u>
Witching On A Star
As You Witch
Witch You Were Here
Just Witch It
Summer Witchin'

<u>**Children of the Fallen**</u>
Death In Her Eyes
Fire In Her Blood

The Beast of the Fae Court
Granting Her Wish
Vampire CEO

USA TODAY BESTSELLING AUTHOR
ERIN BEDFORD

UNTIL SUNSET

Chapter 1

THE GLADE WASN'T ANYTHING like I remembered it. It was funny because it hadn't been more than a year since I'd been here. Nothing had changed. It was me. I'd changed.

The sun was brighter, almost blindingly so. The entire place was louder too. What used to be the background noise of sheep baying and cows mooing was now blaring in my ears. It took all my effort just to tune it out.

Oh! And the smell!

Who knew the fields I use to play and work in now stunk of manure and rotting vegetables. The moment we crossed out of Middleton into the Glade, my nose burned from it. I'd have preferred the wretched coal smell.

I was lucky the house my father hid me in was farther away from the fields and closer to the edge of Alban. It didn't eliminate the smell, but it dulled it a bit. I'd rather smell the woods up against the back of the one-room, one-bathroom house in any case.

Most days, I sat in the corner of the room, staring at nothing. My mind reeled, reliving every moment of my conversion. Being tied down to the cold slab of concrete, Patrick hovering over me, the taste of his blood in my mouth. My throat convulsed as I tried to swallow, my hunger reminding me I hadn't fed since I'd been here.

My father left food for me, but while Patrick had told me human food would help with the cravings, they didn't completely stop them. I could feel my stomach trying to eat itself from my lack of feeding, but I refused to use one of the humans in the Glade. They barely had enough nutrition to live themselves. They didn't need me adding to their issues. Besides, I didn't exactly stay around for vampire orientation. I wouldn't know how to wipe their memory, and then I'd have victims claiming there's a monster in their midst.

Might as well put a glowing sign up saying, *Come, kill me!*

Too bad I didn't have that book, *A Guide for the Newly Converted.* It would have come in handy about now. Not that I hadn't read the whole thing back to front, but it didn't compare to the real thing. I was kicking myself for taking off without searching for it in Marsha's room.

My heart clenched painfully at the memory of him, his soft smile, and kind words. I wished all the time that I'd have said something to him before all this. That I hadn't been so dense to notice him noticing me. We might have hit it off and then gotten married, had children, and then neither of us would have been eligible to be elected.

But it was too late for that. I wasn't human anymore, and Marsha didn't even know who I was. He might not even remember who he was before all this. Not like they let me question him during the five minutes I got to see him at my wedding.

My wedding. I snorted. More like the Crimson Fold's way of showing everyone I belonged to them now. That I was one of them.

A series of knocks, first two then a pause before another three, pounded on the door. I stood from the floor and dusted off my pants. Not that it would do any good. The shack I was staying in was filthy, probably because no one had lived in it for a few years. I'd been too consumed in my own misery to bother trying to clean it up. Hopefully, I wouldn't be here long.

I twisted the handle and put on my best 'hanging in there' smile as my father's face came into view. When I saw his strained, worried look, guilt ate at me. It was my fault he had extra lines on his face. That his hair had grayed almost completely. I wished I could blame that on my stepmother, but in this situation, I knew it was me. It was hardly fair. I got to live forever, and he was aging before my very eyes.

"Hey, Clarabelle," he smiled, but it didn't reach his eyes, another thing to add to the list to be guilty about. "How are you holding up?"

I shifted to let him inside the cabin. "I'm alright." I let out a nervous chuckle. "All things considered."

My father nodded. "Understandable." He sat the bag he held on the small table, if you could even call it that. It was more like a wood top being held up by a milk crate. I shut the door and leaned against it, crossing my arms over my chest, watching as he unpacked the care package he always brought with him.

"You didn't get this from ...?" My voice trailed off, waving my hand toward the mixture of fruits and vegetables on the table.

He pulled out a bag of jerky as he turned. "No, of course not." My father shook his head sadly. "These people can barely feed themselves, let alone a fugitive."

I winced at his description, though it was true. We didn't have fugitives often in Alban. Usually, they were caught before they ever got close to the Glade. I wondered if they had sounded the alarm yet, or if they ever would. I'd imagine Patrick and the rest of the Crimson Fold wouldn't want it getting out that one of their own, their poster child for the Core, had gotten away. I was surprised they hadn't hunted me down in the middle of the night to cut my head off. That worry was probably why I hadn't slept well since arriving - or at all.

"So, if you didn't get it from here, where did you get it from?" I asked, trying to get my mind off the possibility of decapitation.

The look on my father's face said everything.

I sighed. "Does she know?"

"No, your stepmother doesn't know. None of them do." He moved away from the makeshift table and placed his hands on my shoulders. "I would never put you at risk like that."

"Yeah, cause we both know none of them can keep a secret to save their lives, let alone mine." I snorted, earning me a frown from him.

"You know, your stepmother only wants what's best for you."

I snorted again and shook my head. "And that's why she told me to do whatever was necessary to keep Patrick happy, so *her* daughters could have a charmed life?" I raised a brow and then sighed. "Face it, she only sees me as a nuisance. She hates the fact that I was invited to the election over Julianna. That I actually won. Sure, it might have given her all the prestige and wealth she could hope for, but it didn't make her care about me any more than she did before."

"Now, that's not true," my father tried to argue. "Belinda talks about you more than you think. Often praises you for your ability to adapt."

I forced myself not to roll my eyes. I was sure anything nice Belinda had to say about me was meant negatively. How my father couldn't see it was beyond me. They didn't have anything in common.

"Do you love her?" I asked suddenly.

My father dropped his arms from my shoulders, surprised by my question. "Of course, I do." I stared at him, my brows up at my hairline until he let out a tired breath. "Clarabelle, you have to understand. When you get to be my age, you make compromises for those you care about."

I didn't mention the fact that I'd never be his age. Instead, I said, "I don't understand. What compromises?"

He took my hands in his, his fingers stroking over the top of them, and his eyes down. "I loved your mother with all my heart." He let out a heavy, gut-wrenching sigh. "And when she passed, you were the only thing keeping me going. The light in the dark so to speak."

A thickness filled my throat as he spoke. He'd never really talked about my mother. It'd always been something taboo in our house. We both missed her so much that thinking of her was too much to handle. It was easier to push her to the back of our minds and forget. Or try to.

"I saw what life in the Glade did to your mother, and what it does to all its residents every day." His eyes moved up to meet mine. "I didn't want that for you. I wanted better."

I saw where this was going even before he said it. "So, you married her to get me out."

A small smile played on his lips. "Belinda was all refinement and poise. I'd see her every time I made a delivery. We would make small talk, usually about our children." His eyes sparkled with amusement. "Then, the next thing I knew, we're having dinner, and we're discussing our late spouses. Even though we had our children, Belinda was just as lonely as I was for companionship. So ..."

"So, you married her." I finished for him, my guilt at an all-time high. How selfish of me to wish he'd never married. To be so caught up in my own misery to never notice the sadness in his face or the loneliness in his eyes. *I'm such a horrible daughter.*

He shrugged as if it didn't matter. "Yes, I married her. I had hoped it would give you a better life and a chance to be a little less lonely as well. I see that didn't work out as I had planned."

"The girls are fine," I said lying through my teeth. "We just don't have much in common is all."

"Ah, I could see that." He grinned down at me fondly, brushing my hair away from my face. "You a farm girl and them from the big city. I'd imagine it would be hard to find something in common."

"Yeah," I murmured as the realization came over me. I told him I didn't have anything in common with my stepsisters, but really, I didn't even know them. Lea, a few years my junior, was funny and might have been a great little sister if I'd spent time with her.

The same with Julianna. We were close to the same age, but I'd let her materialistic personality get in the way of finding out what she was genuinely like. I'd looked down my nose at them from the beginning. And now, I'd never know what it would be like to have real sisters.

I wasn't even bitter about my stepmother's dislike of me anymore. I couldn't be. She was just like my father, trying to do what was best for her children in her own way. But if I was really honest with myself, I didn't feel much of anything besides the unending hunger. Even then, standing there with my father, I had to use all my strength to focus on his words and not the pulsating of the vein in his neck. The blood surged through his body, calling to me.

My teeth ached, and a low rumble came from my throat.

"Whoa!" My father chuckled. "You must be hungry. Why don't you sit down and eat?" He moved over to the table, throwing things together on a plate he'd brought.

I stared down at the food in disgust. Vegetables and meat weren't what I was hungry for. The only thing that would slake my hunger was beneath my father's dry and wrinkled skin. If I could just taste it, it might be enough to hold me over until I could find something else to eat.

"Hey now." My father voice drew me out of the fog I'd been in. I was just a foot from him now, my shoulders hunched as if I were about to pounce on him. I hadn't even realized I'd moved.

My father withdrew the plate with a nervous laugh. "I know it's not the gourmet stuff you had in the capital, but it's some of the best stuff in the Inner Circle." He picked up a piece of the jerky and bit into it. He chewed it around in his mouth and forced a smile. "See? Delicious!"

I swallowed hard forcing my need for blood down. "I'm sure it's great." I took the plate from him and shoved a piece of something in my mouth. I didn't know what it was. It all tasted like ash to me. Nothing would make me feel whole again until I found some blood. I just had to hold out until my father was gone. He was the only thing left I cherished, and I didn't know how long that would last, not when he found out what I'd become.

Chapter 2

MEDICINE IN THE GLADE wasn't as advanced as it was in the Core. In the Core, if I got hurt, all it took was one trip to the infirmary, and I was all healed up. Here though, they didn't have the fancy gadgets or creams that the elite had.

We did have herbs. Lots of herbs that tasted horrible and sometimes worked, and other times ... didn't. There was one herb in particular that our medic would use to help dull pain. It also made you hallucinate vividly, but when you had to have your tooth pulled, or a limb cut off, a few extra distractions were never a problem.

The medic didn't used the opiate often; only when they had to. People became addicted to it, and then, next thing they knew they were stealing the small stores we had of it. If you grew addicted, the withdrawals were said to be even worse than the pain you were trying to avoid in the first place.

Those withdrawals made them unpredictable and easy to spot. I remembered seeing a man going through withdrawals. He had been curled up in a ball against one of the broken-down shacks. His eyes darted all around him, bloodshot and full of paranoia. He shook wildly and sweat secreted from every pore until his clothes were drenched. I imagined the way that man felt was probably about how I felt right now but worse.

After my father left, I watched the light coming through one of the windows, desperate for it to fade, for night to fall so I could leave this piece of crap place and be out in the open air. My fangs ached in my mouth, pressing against my lower lip and just begging for something to sink into.

I held my knees tight against my chest as I moved in a rocking motion. It didn't do much to soothe my thirst, but it distracted me from running out of the shack to attack the first person I saw. It'd be kind of hard to convince the leaders that I meant them no harm if I was feeding on their people.

The food my father had left sat discarded on the table. The taste of it no longer held any appeal and did nothing for my hunger. I could hear the animals moving in the fields just north of me. My hands tightened harder around my legs until the tangy smell of blood touched the air.

Moving my hand away from my leg, I glanced down at my palm. Little half-moons decorated my skin. I watched curiously as the small marks closed and faded almost as quickly as they had appeared.

Well, that was good to know.

If I could heal fast, then it made what I had to do that much easier.

When I looked up from my hand, the sun had set. I stood in a whoosh and had my hand on the door handle before I could process what I'd done. I forced myself to stop and wait. Just because the sun had set didn't mean the Glade was empty. There would still be people out and about, finishing up their chores or just visiting before they each went to their separate homes for the night. As much as I wanted to rip the door off its hinges and find something to sink my teeth into, I had to be patient. I would only be putting myself in danger otherwise.

The last few hours were brutal. I leaned against the shack door just to keep myself from running out. Even worse, when someone got too close to where my little shack stood, I could hear their blood rushing through their veins.

How did Patrick and the others do it? Was the bloodlust weaker at their age? Or was it a constant never-ending need to feed that bogged them down every day? If so, I could kind of see how they could do that to all those people.

I scoffed. Not long ago, I was berating Patrick for having a feeding room. For wiping people so much that they were puppets just so they could feed without issue, and now, here I was, thinking I would do the same. How was I any better than them?

I wasn't, I reminded myself. The Fold made sure to make me into a monster just like them. The difference between them and me was that I wasn't going to let it change me. I wouldn't feed on those unwilling or entranced. In fact, I didn't plan to feed on humans at all.

Blood was blood, right? Animal blood had to be the same thing as human blood. My stomach gurgled in response. I forced myself to ignore it. It was the same thing. Blood was blood.

And if I kept telling myself that, maybe it would be true.

Finally, it was silent outside. Well, not completely. I could still hear some of the animals settling down for the night, and kids yelling in their houses, demanding to stay up one more minute. It was as silent as it was going to get for what I planned to do. Besides, if I didn't find something to eat, I'd be sinking my fangs into myself. I wasn't sure if the whole vampire drinking vampire blood thing worked, but it seemed a bit counterproductive.

The door creaked open, and I winced. I waited for a second, and when no one came running to investigate, I peeked my head out the door. The Glade was draped in gray, the moon and stars the only light to guide those who couldn't see in the dark. Thankfully, one of my newfound abilities included keener eyesight.

I stepped out of the shack and scanned the area around me. The grain field spread out across the area in front of me, the stalks over my head at this time of year. Just about ready to be harvested. It made strolling out of the shack less anxiety-ridden and allowed me to walk at an average speed toward the cattle corral. Of all the animals, I'd figured that the cows would be best able to handle me taking a few nips here and there.

Of course, I saw the irony in me feeding on the cows. Marsha would have pointed a finger at me and said, "See? Cattle."

I shoved Marsha's adorably stern look to the back of my mind where I demanded it stay. I couldn't start a revolution and save everybody if I was starving to death.

Could vampires starve to death?

Shaking the thought off, I focused on my predicament. I'd never hunted before. I was a harvester, maybe even a scavenger. But a hunter? I wouldn't even know where to begin. Did I prowl toward the cow? Come up from behind it? Or did I just jump on it using my super speed and take it by surprise?

Not wanting to psych myself out about it, I decided to just go for it. Maybe my vampire instincts would kick in, and I'd know exactly what I should do. One could only hope.

I approached the corral and leaned against the rusted metal fence holding them inside. The cows shifted and moaned as if they could sense a predator staring them down. I licked my lips, trying to stifle the urge to rip into one of them. Ducking beneath one of the bars, I made a shushing noise, hoping it would calm them down.

Finding a sizeable brown cow, I stroked my hand down her side, cooing to her in a soothing voice. I slid my hand around her neck and dipped my head down, my nose brushing against the line of her neck. She mooed lowly, and it was like I was a different being all together. My heart beat a sultry rhythm as a low rumble tickled the back of my throat. The animal beneath my hands didn't even startle. Instead, she leaned into my touch.

Was this how they did it? Was it this easy to get others to do what they wanted? The feeling was hypnotizing and addicting. I could easily see how the Crimson Fold would become corrupted by its power.

My fangs ached and peeked out from my lips, reminding me of my purpose here. Trying my best not to startle my meal, I gave the cow an extra pat on the head before I reared back and struck. My fangs pierced her flesh and the hot liquid pumping beneath poured out. The cow groaned slightly beneath me but didn't try to get away. The others around us shifted uncomfortably but didn't call attention to us. I wasn't sure if it was because they feared I'd pick them next, or if I had some kind of vampire allure that kept them docile. Either way, it made my feed easier.

I'd been entirely wrong about blood being blood. Human blood was far superior to animal blood. It wasn't disgusting by any means, but it was more like craving a chocolate cake and getting a carrot instead. It would fill my stomach but wasn't wholly satisfying.

When I couldn't drink anymore, I slowly withdrew from the cow. The cow moaned its displeasure, and my eyes sought out the place I'd bitten and saw it was still bleeding. I quickly placed my hand over the wound and tried to staunch the bleeding, but it wouldn't stop.

Panic rushed through me. If the cow kept bleeding, she would die, and then the farmers would notice. If they saw, they'd start to look for the culprit, and I wasn't exactly the perfect criminal about all this. They could easily find me, and then that would lead them back to my father.

Suddenly, a tingle of a memory tickled the corner of my mind. When Patrick bit me the first time, he'd done something. Something to stop the bleeding. What had he done?

My nose wrinkled as I realized what I had to do.

Leaning forward again, I removed my hand from the wound, and my tongue darted out. I licked the two puncture wounds. The hair on the back of the cow brushed my tongue, and I forced myself not to jerk back. This had to be done. If I was going to feed on them, I could at least do them the courtesy of healing them especially since I had the ability now.

When the bleeding slowed, I pulled away to check the wound. The holes I'd left were healed as if I'd never done it in the first place. It'd have been perfect had the blood not stained the cow's neck, but there wasn't much I could do about that. It wasn't bad enough that anyone would notice.

I hoped.

With my stomach full, I didn't immediately head back to my shack. I'd been cooped up for too many hours and just needed to breathe. I knew tomorrow would be another full day of sitting around contemplating what I would do next, something I really didn't want to waste my precious time outside thinking about.

I didn't need to think of where to go. My feet moved on their own. I walked past the fields and animals, away from the group of homes, and toward a secluded section surrounded by trees where we kept the dead. Not many people spent their time in this part of the Glade. Most didn't want to be reminded of the death of their loved ones, but I'd always found a certain solace in seeing the markers for each person who'd passed.

As I stepped into the inner circle, my eyes automatically found my mother's marker. It wasn't much, just a metal circle that had been shoved halfway into the ground. We'd etched her name into it and laid flowers on her grave that day. White peonies had always been her favorite. We couldn't get them in the Glade, but Father had made sure to make a delivery that day so he could buy some from the Inner Circle.

I'd cried harder than I had in my entire life the day we'd laid my mother to rest. My father hadn't. He'd placed his hand on my shoulder and told me it'd be alright, that my mother was in a better place. What place that was, I didn't know, and he'd never explained. I guess it didn't matter now since the likelihood of me ever going there was slim to none.

There were fresh flowers on her grave. I didn't have to guess that my father had put them there. Now that we technically lived in the Inner Circle, he could get white peonies all the time. I was happy to see he hadn't forgotten her though. I wondered if, after I'd lived as long as Patrick, I would forget them, or if I would still come to put flowers on my family's graves?

Did Asher remember his parents, or did Patrick? Did any of them remember what it was like to be human? Some of them seemed so otherworldly that it was hard to imagine they ever had any humanity to begin with.

I sat there at my mother's grave until the stars began to fade and I was forced to go back to my shack. As I curled up into a ball on the floor, I prayed to whatever deity was listening that I could hold onto my humanity for as long as possible.

Chapter 3

THE DAYS THAT FOLLOWED began to blur together. I'd spent the day in the shack, not waking until the afternoon when my father would show up with food for me. I'd go through the motions of eating and making small talk with him. Then I would sneak out of my shack, find some animal to feed on - I never fed on the same one twice - and then spend the rest of the night walking around the Glade. Sometimes, I'd sit at my mother's grave telling her all about what happened to me, other times, I'd just sit in silence.

I still hadn't come clean about what happened to me, and I knew my father suspected something was different. But how did you explain the monster you'd become to the only person who still loved you? Could I really be blamed for wanting to hold onto him for as long as I could?

I knew when he found out he'd look at me differently. When I'd found out about Patrick, I hadn't precisely reacted well, not that he had been open about it to begin with. I hoped my father would at least let me explain before pulling out the pitchforks.

I knew I'd have to come clean soon. Someone was bound to notice my activities, and my father wasn't stupid. The problem was I wasn't sure what to tell him. Did I flash my fangs and say, "Hey, I'm a vampire now. You know about them, right?"

I didn't see that ending well.

After filling him in on what I was, and what the Crimson Fold really did, I still had the problem of telling the rest of Alban. My father might be easy to convince, but strangers were more likely to kill first, ask questions later. Not that they'd know how to kill me if I didn't tell them. How likely would someone go straight for the head or heart anyway?

My inner monologue was interrupted by the sound of voices close to my shack. I tensed where I sat, staying as still as possible. Had someone found out I'd been staying there? Had they noticed my feeding patterns? I was in for it now. I just knew it.

I'd learned quickly to block out the surrounding noises. Otherwise, they gave me a headache. Try sleeping with the entire world blaring in your ear. Not pleasant at all, I can tell you. I closed my eyes and focused on the muffled voices to hear what they had to say.

"Come on, Willa," a male voice coaxed, his voice a low tone. "Just for a little bit."

Willa, I assumed, giggled. "No, we're supposed to be checking the grain count. If the overseer finds out that we're messing around instead, we'll get a lashing." There was some more giggling and then a smacking of lips before they moved away from my shack. I could relax again.

The mention of my father made me frown. We didn't dole out punishments often, but when we did, they weren't likely to forget it. I'd never been on the other side of the whip, but I'd seen many public lashings over my seventeen years. There was one instance that stuck out the most in my mind.

When I was nine, a boy not much older than myself had stolen from the stores that were set to go to the Inner Circle. The authorities had dragged him into the middle of our little development. His clothes, like many of us, were ragged; his cheeks not as filled in as they would have been if he had lived in the Inner Circle. I remembered thinking his hair was the color of the wheat I'd helped cut down that day.

There was already a red mark on the side of his face when they tied him down to a pole that sat in the middle of the village square. He cried and screamed for his mother, his father, anyone who would save him. A woman responded to his cries with her own as she pushed through the crowd. Her hair matched that of the boy's and had to be his mother. Several men held her back, not allowing her to go to her child.

I remembered thinking, *Just let her go to him. He's obviously scared.* But I hadn't dared to voice those thoughts. I was too young and too frightened myself to speak out. Not like now. The memory of the scathing remarks I'd made to the Crimson Fold during my interview session came to mind.

I snorted. How naive I'd been to think that I'd be able to stop anything back then. I couldn't have even saved myself, let alone anyone else.

The only thing that had come to mind at that moment was to find my father. I'd searched for my father's face in the crowd that had gathered. His face had never been colder than at that very moment, and for the first time in my life, I was afraid of him. When he'd seen me looking at him, his stony expression melted for a moment, and I'd seen the regret there. But, then, as if it had never happened, it was gone. He hadn't wanted to do it either. That somehow had made me hurt more for him than for the child.

Watching in my growing horror, I'd seen them hand my father the whip. His hand had tightened around the handle, the length of it sitting in his other hand. He hadn't moved right away, his breathing coming in slow movements. It was almost like he had to psych himself up for it. I knew I would have.

My eyes followed my father as he walked toward the child. Observing him had been one of the horrific moment of my life next to my mother's death. The closer he'd gotten to him, the louder the mother's cries were, and even the rest of the crowd began to shift in displeasure. No one liked to see a child hurt, but none of them would stop him.

Before he could get to the boy, a man, about the same age as my father, ran out.

Two of my father's men had stopped him from approaching, but he said something I couldn't hear that had caused my father to let him come closer. They'd spoken for a moment in low quick tones. My father had glanced at the boy and then back toward man. He'd said something else I couldn't make out, and the man nodded, a determined look on his face.

The next thing I knew, the boy had been released and the man had taken his place. The boy didn't get to go back to his family. He had to stand a few feet away from his father and watch as my father whipped him. Over and over again, the whip slashed through the air, the crack of it had filled my ears and nightmares for days.

The man never cried out, never begged him to stop. He just took the punishment while his family protested nearby. No one had moved to help him. They all knew the penalty for stealing. It had been ingrained in us since we were small. We get a set number of rations for our family. No more. No less. If you were still hungry, tough. Go chew on some grass. That was about the only option you had.

By the time my father had let the whip go limp in his hand, the man's back was covered in bloody red ribbons, and he

34

collapsed against the pole. The child had stopped trying to get to him and sank to the ground, his face red and blotchy from crying. I remembered thinking his father must have been stupid, or loved him too much, to let him take the punishment. After that day, the boy never stole again and that many more people were reminded of the price of stealing.

I also learned a sound lesson that day, but not about stealing. I learned why I'd always been seen as different. Even though I had been standing in the crowd with the rest of them, even though my face had been covered in tears as well, I didn't get the same recognition. The adults didn't punish me the same as the others if I spoke out of turn, and the children didn't invite me to play with them.

I didn't blame them. I understood. I really did. After all, would you want to be friends with the girl whose father punished yours?

Being the child I had been, I'd complained to my father. Why did he have to be the one to do it? Why couldn't the Crimson Fold dish out the punishments? It was their job, wasn't it?

My father's answer was alway, "I'm in charge. It is my responsibility." Like that answered my questions at all.

Now that I was older, I understood more. Having power didn't mean you could always avoid unpleasant moments. That there wouldn be things you didn't want to do but had to. As I bit into the goat I'd chosen for my meal that night, I felt that lesson more than I'd ever felt it before. Even the lesson about friends had followed me.

It wasn't until I'd moved to the Inner Circle that I'd even gained a real friend, and even those had strayed when I won the election. The servants didn't look at me the same way they looked at Marsha or Violet. Violet had also started to see me differently. Marsha and Narq had been the only ones who hadn't had their perceptions of me change. They hadn't treated me like whatever they said to me would go back to Patrick and get them in trouble. Naturally, because I'd tried to run away with them.

I wiped my mouth with the back of my hand and briefly worried that Narq had ended up in the dungeon along with Tillie. I made a mental note that if I ever got the chance to get them out, I would. I might not be able to save everyone, but I'd save who I could. Even if I couldn't protect myself.

My mind full of heavy thoughts, I made my way back toward the shack. I didn't feel like talking to my mother today or exploring the Glade. Though my eyes weren't tired, my heart couldn't take anymore. I just wanted to curl up in my corner and brood.

When I saw my shack a few feet away, I froze. The door was open. A light colored the entrance in a golden hue. Someone was in my hiding place. But who? Only my father and I knew I was here, right? Had someone found my hiding spot?

It was hard to believe my father was visiting me this late. He probably figured I'd be sleeping. Plus, he had his own work to do early in the morning, and he undoubtedly favored his sleep over checking up on me.

All these thoughts swirled through my mind as I crept slowly toward the doorway. I paused just outside. I inhaled deeply, testing the air for any sign of who it might be. The familiar scent that filled my lungs made me relax, but only slightly.

I gripped the side of the door and walked into the shack. My father sat with his back against the wall, his brow furrowed as he stared down at the floor. The floor creaked underneath my feet, and his head jerked up. The moment his eyes landed on me, I knew something was wrong.

Chapter 4

"FATHER?" I FORCED MY voice to be steady even though my heart beat rapidly in my chest. A million things ran through my mind as I contemplated what he could possibly be doing here.

My father didn't move from his spot but stared at me. Like really looked at me. His eyes scrutinized my whole form until they settled on my face. The confusion and suspicion in his eyes only caused my anxiety to rise.

"What happened to you?"

The question caught me off guard. I turned away from him to close the door to the shack and give myself a moment to think of an answer. What the heck was I going to tell him? I hardly felt like he cared to hear about the primping and waxing I'd gone through when I arrived at the Core. I cringed inwardly at just the thought of it.

"I'm not sure what you mean," I answered, smacking my hands against the side of my legs. I forced myself to meet my father's gaze, though everything in me told me to look away.

My father pushed to his feet, a bit slower than I expected from someone his age, and I reached out to help him up. He waved me off and stood as far from me as he could. That didn't bode well.

"I know I wasn't able to be there before you were taken to the Core for the election." I opened my mouth to tell him it was okay, but he held his hand up. "I know you understand, but still it upsets me when I was not able to be there for you, especially when you needed me."

"But you showed up later," I reminded him of the time he showed up during one of the nights of the election. "And though I might have sent you off, I did appreciate your coming to see me." I frowned and tilted my head to the side. "Even if it was because of someone unpleasant."

"Which you never explained. Why did they want you out of the election?" My father raised a brow as if it were the most ridiculous thing he'd ever heard of.

I made a face. "Politics as usual. Zara, the mayor's daughter, wanted to be chosen by Patrick and saw me as her number one competition." I sniffed and smirked. "I guess she was right."

"Yes, I suppose so," he mused though he didn't smile. "That doesn't answer my first question."

I shifted uncomfortably. For once, I wished I had the years of practice Patrick and the others had. The effortlessness that let them seem like mobile statues. It would definitely have come in handy right about now.

Sighing, I scuffed my boot on the ground and then glanced up at him, hoping the look I gave him was innocent. "What do you want to know?"

"I want to know what happened to my daughter." His tone was stern and almost to the point of yelling. "I want to know why, out of the blue on her wedding day, she sends a message begging me to save her. No explanation, no nothing. Did that Blordril hurt you? Did he ...?" My father trailed off as if he couldn't bring himself to say what he was thinking.

"No, no. Nothing like that." I quickly reassured him though it was partly a lie. Patrick had hurt me but not in the way he was thinking. The idea of Patrick wanting me that way, even though I was still angry with him, sent a strange kind of warmth into the pit of my stomach.

"Then what? Explain to me because I don't get it." When I was silent, he took a step toward me, and I forced myself to stand still. He grabbed me by the shoulders and shook me slightly. "What are you so afraid of?"

I laughed and not a pleasant one. "Not the things you are thinking."

"You don't want to know what I'm thinking." He shook his head sadly, releasing me with a drop of his arms. "The things I stay up and imagine at night, that could have possibly had you running for the hills?" He sighed heavily and let out a dark chuckle. "There are no words to describe them."

"You're right," I told him, making him look up. "There are no words to describe the horrors I have witnessed, but none of those compare to anything you could have imagined safe in your bed at night."

"But I—"

I held my hand up cutting him off. "No, I'm telling you." I laughed again, shaking my head in disbelief. "I didn't even believe it at first. I hardly believe it now. So, there is no way that you would ever guess it. Not in your wildest nightmares."

My father swallowed visibly, his eyes settled on me. "I can take it. If you can, then I can."

I dropped my gaze first. Not because I was scared, but because I couldn't think of how to start. Every conversation that I'd had about this had ended badly. There had to be a better way to handle this, a better way to explain the monsters that ruled over us. The monster standing before him now.

"Have you heard of how Alban began?" I asked finally, trying to start slowly instead of jumping into it right away. "I mean the real story."

My father's brows furrowed, and he crossed his arms over his chest. "After the wars that decimated everything, the remainder of the human race gathered together under a council of leaders to create what we are now, Alban."

I smiled bitterly. "Close but a bit watered down from the true version."

"What? How do you know this?" He turned his head to the side, searching me for some sign of an answer.

"The election wasn't all about pretty ball gowns and fancy dances, you know." I arched a brow. "I did some reading—" The surprised expression on my father's face made me bark a laugh. "Yes, I know. Me? Reading? Not exactly my cup of tea, but sometimes, reading is all that you have to find the answers you need."

"So, these answers, what were they? What were you looking for?"

"I didn't go searching for answers at first," I explained. "All I was thinking about was getting out of there. Of going home. The last thing on my mind was being the hero of Alban."

"Hero? That's what you plan on being?" Real concern etched into my father's face. "You think you can save us from poverty? From ourselves? How exactly do you think you can do that sitting around here?"

"I don't," I snapped. "Poverty and starvation are the least of your worries. There is something far worse that has been hiding right under our noses." I scoffed and corrected myself. "Rather, above our heads." I met my father's confused gaze and made sure my voice was sturdy and strong. "The ones you have to fear are those who rule us. Those who have been here longer than me, longer than you. Heck, before Alban even existed."

"Clarabelle, what are you talking about? That's impossible." He shook his head, his eyes wide. "The Crimson Fold hasn't been around for that long."

"Haven't they?" I asked, urging him to come to the conclusion I wanted on his own. "Have we ever had an election? For the main council, I mean? Patrick has been the leader since I was born, and he looks no older now he did then. Tell me? Is that just good genes?"

"His father must have—"

"Looked exactly like him?" I finished for him with a hint of disbelief. "I hate to break it to you, but the Crimson Fold? They are the same as the day Alban came to be. Patrick is the same leader who pulled us out of chaos and gave us order."

"No, that's not possible." My father began to pace, rubbing a hand over his face. He stopped for a moment and stared at the wall. I waited. Waited for him to find the words that he needed to hear. The ones that he didn't want to believe. The ones I wished never had to come to life.

"Is it possible?" my father finally asked, turning to me. "Tell me it's not possible. That this is all a joke."

"It gets worse."

He laughed then. A deep dark laugh that came from his belly. "Of course, it does." Sinking down to the ground, he leaned over his knees, his head hanging down. "Might as well give it to me all at once."

I took a deep breath and gave it to him as he asked. "Vampires. They're vampires."

My father's head whipped up. "Vampires? Are you sure?"

It was my turn to be confused. I'd expected him to plow me with questions. What's a vampire? How do you kill them? And so on, but not: "Are you sure?"

"You've heard of vampires?" I asked, slowly making sure to put emphasis on the word vampires.

"Yes, well. I've heard whispers. Tales you told your children to make them behave." The expression on my face made him stop. "Not that I told you any of those. You weren't the kind of child that needed to be scared into obedience."

I snorted. "Maybe you should have."

"Anyway," he drew out with a frown. "I'd never paid much attention to the stories, I had other things to worry about." He raised his brow as if it said everything.

"So, what do you know about them?" I pried, hoping he had some information that I didn't. I'd be surprised if he did, but wouldn't that have been lucky?

"Not much." He shrugged, the gesture strange on my father. A forty-three-year-old should not be shrugging. "They don't age, and they drink blood."

"That's it?" My brows raised up into my hairline. "That is the whole of your knowledge about vampires?" When he nodded, all my hope went out the window. If this place had windows. Licking my lips, I sighed. "Okay, so the blood and the not aging is right, but there's a lot more."

"Like what?"

I explained to him everything I had learned so far about the vampires. From my time in the Core, the book for the newly converted, and my firsthand experiences. Not that I had much. I'd only been a vampire for about a week. I was playing it all by ear. If there were more abilities I didn't know about, then they weren't showing up on their own.

"And you are saying Patrick Blordril and the rest of the Crimson Fold are all vampires?" My father asked, a hint of disbelief still in his voice. I didn't blame him. I wished it wasn't true either.

"Yes, but not just the Fold members." I waved a hand in front of me to stop him from asking more. "My guide, the guy who helped dress me for the balls, he's a vampire, and who knows how many others." Saying it out loud made me realize how little I knew about the occupants of the Core. I knew of thirteen vampires including myself, not including Marsha since I wasn't sure if he had been converted yet, but there had to be more. Right?

"Okay, so we're being controlled by vampires." He wiped the top of his lip with his fingers and then clucked his tongue. "But if they were feeding on us, why wouldn't we have heard about it? There haven't been any disappearances. Unexplained deaths."

I stared at him. Willing him to figure it out. When he seemed like he wasn't ever going to get there, I stepped in. "It's pretty obvious when you think about it. They send invitations out to specific people. Young people, who are all attractive, and within a certain age range. Then some of those people come back, and others don't."

My father's expression went from grim, to shocked, to horrified. He scrambled to his feet, his finger shaking in the air. "You're telling me the election. The whole thing is a big cover up for them to feed on our children?"

I nodded.

The rage that came out from my father was unlike anything I'd ever seen before. He shouted and kicked the side of the makeshift table, toppling it over. Pacing the floor once more, he muttered to himself. Finally, when it didn't look like his anger would abate on its own, I stepped in front of his path and put my hands up.

"Stop. Please. It wasn't your fault. You didn't know. Nobody did." I grabbed his shoulders when he tried to argue. "You. Didn't. Know."

"But I let you," - he cupped my face, tears brimming in his eyes - "my only child, go into that den of monsters. You're right. Nothing I could have imagined was even close to the horrors you must have faced." He wiped the back of his hand over his eyes. "No wonder you wanted to leave."

I let out a deep breath. Now the moment of truth. The part that would decide if my father could accept me in any form, monster and all.

"There's something else I need to tell you." I swallowed and blinked several times. "That night. The night of my wedding." I stepped back from him, making sure there was a bit of distance between us, the violent display I'd just witnessed still clear in my mind.

"What? What is it?" my father came toward me, but I held a hand up to stop

49

him. He growled and stomped his foot. "Just tell me."

Instead of saying the words, I opened my mouth, letting my fangs slip between my lips. My father didn't say anything at first. He didn't even seem to respond. But then he blinked and uttered one word, "Oh."

Chapter 5

MY FATHER LEFT IN a hurry after my confession. Not that I didn't understand. If he had come to me saying that he was one of the monsters I'd heard of growing up, I'd have done more than rush out the door.

Oh, wait. I did do that.

As I laid down for the day, I thought about the final night of the election. Patrick had been so charming then. I mean, he was still charming now, but I knew how dangerous he actually was. I'd been so determined to leave that my affection for him had caught me by surprise. Then he took my first kiss and warped it, turning into the monster I'd never known I should have feared.

I imagined that would be my last kiss ever. Not unless Marsha accepted me for the way I was now or by some miracle I forgave Patrick. Some part of me knew it wasn't his fault. He was shoved into a corner, he didn't have a choice, but still, if I had the choice between dying and becoming a vampire ... well, I wasn't sure.

I'd love to say I was righteous enough to say, "No, I'd rather die," but I was also selfish enough to want to live, no matter the cost.

A bang on the door of the shack made my eyes snap open. I sat upright, the light filtering in through the cracks of the shed. It was morning already? When had I fallen asleep?

I didn't have time to get up or make myself presentable before the door to the shack was thrown open. Frozen against the wall, I waited for the intruder to come into my hiding spot, but when my father's face appeared, I instantly relaxed.

"What's wrong?" I asked, sitting up. "You don't usually come this early."

He didn't answer me right away but pulled the door shut and sighed, his back still to me. When he turned around, the expression on his face could only be described as cautious. Was my father afraid of me? That was something I'd never hoped to see.

"I'm sorry, Clara," he started, calling me by my nickname. He never called me Clara. It was always Clarabelle. It was only when he was trying to soften the blow of something that he used the shorter version of my name. I wasn't sure what he was apologizing for, but I was already worried.

"You don't have anything to be sorry for." I stood up and took a step toward him.

He moved back, and I stopped. Well, that answered it. He was afraid of me. I leaned against the wall on the opposite side of the shack and waited. The only way I'd be able to get us both through this was to go at his pace. After all, I had forever.

My father shifted near the door, shame on his face, probably because of his reaction to me. I wanted to reassure him, but this was something I couldn't help him with, no matter how much I wanted to.

"I wanted to apologize for my reaction yesterday." He coughed and shuffled his feet, crossing his arms over his chest. "I was just taken by surprise. All this talk about monsters and vampires, and I never expected my daughter to be one of them."

My foot moved forward on its own, and I opened my mouth to explain, but he held his hand up, a pleading look in his eyes.

"Please, don't. It's not that I'm worried you'll hurt me, I just need time to process all this." He rubbed his hand over his face and then dropped it to his side. "I just want to know one thing."

"Of course." I shook my head slightly. "Ask me anything."

"Why?"

My brows furrowed, and I cocked my head to the side. "Why?"

He finally moved away from the wall and came toward me, his arms opened to me. "Why would you want to do this to yourself? Why would you want to live forever?"

I snort-laughed. And then I honestly laughed. I leaned over, my hands on my knees, trying to catch my breath from laughing so hard. When I stood back up, my father did not seem amused.

"I don't see how this is at all funny. Becoming a vampire is a serious matter. You can't ever age. Have children. You'll always have to hide from those around you."

Clearing my throat, I said with a solemn tone, "I know, which is why I didn't ask for this."

"You didn't?" My father's eyes widened a fraction. "Then how did this happen?" He gestured to me with a hand.

I sniffed. "How do you think? They knocked me out, tied me down, and forced me to change."

My father was quiet for a moment the look on his face scary even to me. His voice came out low and threatening as he said, "Who did this to you?"

I started to tell him it was Patrick, but something stopped me. I closed my mouth and then opened it again, my head turned away from him. "I don't know. I woke up like this."

For a moment, I thought he wouldn't believe me, but then suddenly, he pulled me into his embrace. I tensed at first before letting my arms wrap around him. Inhaling him deeply, I let myself sink into the comfort he was offering. After all was said and done, I wasn't sure when I'd get to - if ever - hug my father like this again.

Withdrawing from me, my father looked down on me as if searching for something.

"What is it?" I reached up to touch my cheek. "Do I have something on my face?"

"No." He chuckled and cupped my cheeks. "I just was expecting there to be more of a difference in you. Something that screamed I'm a vampire. I'm happy you still look like you." He sighed and dropped his hands. "Though, I have to say I'm a little disappointed."

"Disappointed?"

He lifted a shoulder. "Well, yes. How else are we going to be able to tell who's a vampire and who isn't? I hardly think they are all going to let us hold them down and look at their teeth." The grim smile on his face wasn't reassuring.

"I get what you mean." My tongue slid across my own fangs before I realized I had done it. Forcing my tongue to stay where it belonged, I shifted my weight from one foot to the other. "Is that all you came here for? To confirm you hadn't been dreaming?" I offered him a small smile, trying to lighten the mood. When he didn't return my smile, I frowned. "Father?"

He seemed to close in on himself, his shoulders hunching and his hand going up to grip the back of his neck. He wouldn't meet my gaze as he said, "Some of the herders have come to me about something attacking the animals."

I swallowed hard and went for innocent until proven guilty. "Attacking them? Like what?"

My father shrugged. "I don't know. There were no wounds, just dried blood in their fur. So, either they are being healed, or someone is just dumping blood on them." He made an impatient sound. "What I don't get is that it's completely random. There was a cow a few days ago, a goat after, and then a sheep. Now, this morning they have said another cow has been marked."

"And you came to ask me what I thought about it?" I raised a brow forcing myself to stay calm and not panic.

"No, not exactly." He grimaced and then let out a heavy sigh. "The attacks started around the time I brought you here."

"So, you thought it had something to do with me?" I asked, making sure my voice sounded unsure and not accusing.

"Well, Clarabelle." He huffed. "I didn't know what to think. This was before I knew you were, you know …" He gestured at me and then started to pace. "I hadn't come to accuse you of messing with the animals. I just wanted to know if you knew something, or if there was some kind of thing in the Core that would make you do it. Now that I know you're a vampire, I'm thinking the blood on the animals wasn't a prank." His eyes bore into me, but I didn't shrink away from it.

Standing tall, my shoulders back and head held high, rage surged through my veins. I snarled, baring my fangs, "I'm a vampire. I feed on blood. Would you rather I grab one of the villagers? One of my childhood friends? Or maybe I could take blood from those you punish, then you wouldn't have to make a public spectacle about it." Anger colored my words as my blood pumped through my veins. I didn't know what I looked like just then, but whatever it was, it terrified my father.

His mouth dropped open, and he stumbled back from me. When I realized my mistake, I took a deep breath and sank back against the opposite wall. "I'm sorry. I'm still getting used to this." I waved a hand to myself. "Everything is heightened, more extreme. Emotions. Wants. Needs. Everything. I didn't mean to come at you like that."

My father cleared his throat and nodded curtly. "I understand. It's fine. It's fine." He licked his lips, and his eyes darted to the side before moving back to settle on me. "I get that you need to feed, and of course, I wouldn't want you to feed on the villagers. I'll just tell the herders it's a new kind of tick or something."

"I appreciate that."

We exchanged a nod and then fell into an uncomfortable silence. It was strange. I'd never been so out of place with my own father. Once upon a time, I'd have said he was my best friend in the world. That he was the only one who understood me. But now? We were nothing more than strangers. I didn't see an outcome for this intended uprising that ended with a happily ever after … for either of us.

My father finally broke the silence. "What are you going to do now?" I glanced over at him. He tucked his hands into the pockets of his brown pants. "You are out of the Core, and as far as I can tell, no one is looking for you." When I raised a brow, he added, "Believe me, I checked and checked. I even asked your stepmother if she's heard any news of you, and she's had nothing but good things to say. Of course, she's also distracted by Lea's latest admirer." He snorted bitterly. "They don't even know what is going on underneath their noses. That all their good fortune is because we sold you to the monsters."

"You did no such thing," I interrupted him before he could start a pity party. "Sure, it might seem that way, but it wasn't you who put me on that list. I wasn't supposed to be on the list in the first place."

"What?" His brows shot up to his hairline.

My lips twisted into a wry grin. "Apparently, I'm special. A girl from the Glade mixed in with the chosen cattle to be sacrificed to our gods." I muttered the last bit, something I'd been thinking about to myself lately. Shaking off those thoughts, I continued, voice stronger and clearer, "Patrick and his cousin - my guide - Asher planned this. They wanted me to be chosen. The game was fixed from the beginning."

"But why? That doesn't make sense." My father shook his head, and I understood his sentiment. I still didn't understand it all. "Why choose someone they know isn't going to keep quiet?"

"Because they want me to stop it." My words were profound and confident because I'd heard them over and over the last few months. I was the one that was supposed to stop the Crimson Fold. The one who would make everything better. But of course, that still brought the question of how.

"That doesn't make much sense either. Why would the vampires want you to stop them?" My father voiced the same questions I'd have myself. "Are you sure you have it right?"

I nodded. "Yes. Patrick and Asher don't agree with the way the other Fold members behave. Like we don't matter at all. We're just ants to them. They want me to help change that."

"But how?"

It was my turn to shrug. "They never were clear on that part. Just told me to trust them." I scoffed and kicked my boot against the ground. "Look where that got me."

"So, what are you going to do now?"

I had been rash to take off without finding out the full extent of what we were up against. All I had was myself and my word. Both of those things would be dangerous to just present to the world. My father might be forgiving, but the rest of them? I wasn't so sure. I needed more information. At least, know how many vampires there are.

With my decision made, I glanced back up from the floor and met his gaze. "The only thing I can do. I have to go back."

Chapter 6

GETTING OUT OF THE Core was a lot easier than getting back into it. I couldn't ride along with my father for a delivery because he didn't have any. I also didn't want him anywhere near the Core. I didn't want to give them an excuse to use him as leverage against me.

I chuckled to myself as I darted across the darkened fields. A year ago, the idea of my father being leverage against me wouldn't even have crossed my mind. If anything, I'd have been his weakness. Someone they could bully to make him do their bidding, but I half wanted someone to do that now. I'd rip their heads off their bodies and deliver it to their families in a neatly wrapped box.

Whoa. I forced myself to clear the image from my mind. That was dark. I'd always had a pretty vivid imagination but decapitating someone had never been on my list of daydreams. Was Patrick's blood making me crueler? Or was it there all along and the vampire in me had just brought it to the surface?

I didn't let myself contemplate that prospect for long. I had other, more important things to worry about. Like how to get out of the Glade undetected.

There were four sections to the Glade, one for each point of the compass. My father oversaw the southern side. Each side also had only one way into Middleton. That entrance had guards with high powered weapons that would blow a hole through my chest. I'd seen it happen. Not a pretty picture.

The wall between the Glade and Middleton was a lot larger than that of the Core and the Inner Circle, probably because they didn't expect those in the Inner Circle to want to escape. If anything, they'd be trying to get into the Core, not out of it. That was probably why it was so easy for me to get out.

I almost got caught by a few stragglers on their way home. I could only thank the tall stalks of grain in the fields that I was able to hide between, keeping me from their view. I watched them as they passed, my eyes trained on them.

Two men. Not much larger than my father. They were talking about the counts for the day. Boring stuff. Things that would have put me to sleep at a different time.

"Man," one of the men cried out, looking down at his hand. "That thing really got me."

"You need to be more careful," the other man chastised him. "You don't want to get an infection."

The injured man grimaced.

If I hadn't had such good eyesight, I might not have seen it. As it were, they were as clear as day to me. I could see every facial expression and movement, even the wrap around the injured man's hand. Red colored the white fabric, and I tensed.

My nostrils flared at the hint of blood in the air. My feet moved forward of their own accord. I hadn't fed tonight, there wasn't time. Didn't matter really, the animal blood didn't quite satisfy the thirst for real, warm human blood. My fangs ached as I got closer to them. My foot cracked on a fallen stalk, making the two men freeze.

"What was that?" The other man's eyes shot to my hiding spot. I stayed as still as possible though my fangs ached to sink into his friend's hand.

The injured man shook his head and kept moving. "It's probably just a cat or something. Come on, I need to get some stitches in this thing. Think the medic has some of those pain-killing herbs left?"

The other man didn't move his gaze from where I stood, his eyes searching for something. Finally, after what seemed like forever, he turned away from where I hid and started after his friend.

Smacking him on the back, the uninjured one said, "You know they won't give it to you unless you're dying. A nick on the hand isn't dying. Suck it up."

"You don't know my pain," the injured one complained, and his friend laughed.

I listened to them as they moved further and further away, my stomach growling at me for letting them go. I didn't blame it. Working on an empty stomach was never good, but I wasn't about to blow my cover by jumping the first person with a cut.

When I was sure I was in the clear, I crept from my spot and, in a whoosh, found myself pressed up against the inner wall. My speed still surprised me even though I'd had it for a while now. I'd never been a fast runner, nor a slow one. Anytime we had to exercise for school, I'd be in the middle of the pack. Just average. Nothing special.

Now, though, I'd leave them in the dust, even lap them a few times. The speed definitely was one of the better parts of my new condition.

No one sounded the alarm as I made my way across the wall. It was too tall for me to attempt jumping. Even my abilities had their limits. Plus, the spikes on top would hurt if I landed wrong. Impaled on steel spikes was never high on my ways to die list.

With going over a no go and a seeming lack of tunneling abilities to go under the wall, I had to go through the only gate. The heavily guarded gate. Oh, joy.

As I approached the well-lit archway, I hid behind a work shed. There were two guards as usual, with none on the other side. If I could draw them away somehow, I might be able to sneak through. I had super speed. If now wasn't the time to utilize it, I didn't know when would be.

I glanced around me to see what I had to work with. There was a barrel with some pitchforks. I shuddered at the sight of them. The likelihood of me ending up on the wrong end of those was too close for comfort. Besides a few other farming tools - which wouldn't really help me out in this situation, unless I planned to seed them to death - the only other things possibly useful were some large rocks.

Sighing, I reached down and grabbed one of them. *Beggars can't be choosers*, I thought as I hurled it a few yards away from the guards.

Immediately, their heads jerked up and turned toward the sound. They didn't move away from the entrance and, after a moment, settled back into position. I threw another one and then another one.

On that third throw, they ran toward the sound, shouting, "Hey, you there!"

Taking my chance, I rushed from behind the shed. I almost hesitated at the bright light filling the area around the entrance but forced myself to keep going as I made it through the open gate and into Middleton. I heard the guards coming back, so I quickly ducked between some metal structures.

With the Glade behind me and one step closer to the Core, I could relax a bit. No one in Middleton knew me, not unless they had seen me on the monitors, but from what I'd heard, the Moles had even less time than we did to watch those.

My nose wrinkled. The air here was thicker and had a tinge of coal particles to it. I wasn't sure if vampires needed to breathe to live, but since it didn't make me immediately go into a coughing fit, I assumed I was safe, at least from dying, if not from the smell.

I'd only been to Middleton once before. When I was ten, we had a field trip to tour Alban. Something about making sure we understood how important our part was in the workings of the whole country. All it did was show me how less fortunate we were than those in the Inner Circle. Thinking about it now, that was probably what the Crimson Fold wanted, to pit us against each other and make us resent those they have favored.

I snorted. Little did they know.

My eyes scanned the dusty area. Where the Glade was green and full of life, Middleton was a world of gray. The buildings were cold, hard metal of different shades of gray, some rusted beyond repair. The ground wasn't much better. Where we had grass and sometimes pretty flowers, there wasn't any sign of life. Dirt and gravel decorated the ground.

The most significant difference was the silence.

In the Glade, we worked in the fields or with the animals. So, there was some form of talking or sometimes even singing as we worked, but in Middleton, there was no sign of ... anybody. No children playing. No workers.

Of course, it was after work hours, but even in the Glade, there were stragglers. I could barely hear the hearts beating in the metal shacks. Were they so much more repressed here than we were? It was hard to believe, but it was possible. I wouldn't want to live in Middleton, working underground, rarely getting to see the sky. It seemed like a horrible way to live ... if you'd call breathing in this filth living.

Walking down the obvious path, my eyes scanned around me. I didn't believe I would get through the whole section before coming across someone. It would be too easy.

Then, as if reading my mind, a woman came stumbling out of one of the houses. She coughed and fell to her knees, coughing harder. No one went out of their homes to check on her. If anything, Middleton became quieter, as if the entire

69

population was holding their collective breath.

The woman's coughing turned into a fit. She braced herself on the ground and gagged. Thick black gunk spilled out of her mouth and fell to the earth, and I looked away. I'd never had a strong stomach. Just the sight of vomit usually made me want to throw up as well. I looked away until it sounded like she was done, but when my eyes went back to her, she had collapsed on the ground. I almost walked away but stopped. She wasn't moving.

My feet quickly moved toward her, and I knelt beside her, being careful not to kneel in the vomit. Her hair was thrown over her face, and I pushed it back to check the pulse on her neck. At first, I thought she just had dark skin, but soon realized it was dirt or coal dust. It was so ingrained in her skin that she probably couldn't get it out anymore.

I glanced down at my hands. They were clean and perfectly manicured. Not how they were when I first arrived in the Core. Back then, my fingers had been like hers, except mine was from digging and planting in the fields rather than working in the mines. When I first met Asher, they had soaked my hands in some kind of solution that had removed all traces of my home, leaving behind only what they wanted to see.

Brushing the thought away, I felt her pulse. Nothing. She'd coughed herself to death. Probably inhaled too much coal dust or whatever other horrid things filled the air here. I stared down at her. I wanted to be sad. I really did, but I was just tired. The revolution hadn't even started yet, and I was ready for it to be over.

I sniffed and shook my head. What did that say about our chance?

No one came out to collect the body. It probably happened too often for them to care. I glanced back at the woman, wondering if there was anything I could do. I didn't have anything with me to clean her up with. I didn't even know how they gave burials here. Even if I had a whole vat of that cleaning stuff, I didn't think it would bring the woman back to life.

Not that it would do any good. She'd just end up breathing in more of the stuff and die all over again. Sometimes, there was really nothing you could do. Sometimes, the only option available was to walk away. Which was what I did. I stood up, dusted my pants off, and walked away, not looking back, no matter how much I wanted to.

Chapter 7

THE WALL SEPARATING MIDDLETON and the Inner Circle was identical to that of the one around the Glade, except there were a lot more guards. Apparently, not a whole lot of people wanted to get into Middleton, but a lot more wanted into the Inner Circle. With what I'd just seen, I could understand why.

I didn't trust that I could use the same trick I did on the other guards. Two guards were easy to fool. Four? Not so much.

Instead of heading toward the gate, I searched along the line of the wall for some way over. There was a rickety old structure that must have been a watchtower at some point, but now it looked like it might fall over at any moment. The ladder had broken off halfway up, probably another factor as to why the guards didn't care much about it.

Hazardous to humans. Not so much for vampires.

I crept over to the structure, my eyes locked on where the guards stood. The light was busted over here, so I was cloaked in shadows. Unless one of them was an owl or I made a lot of noise, they wouldn't find me.

Placing a foot on the bottom support beam of the tower, I lifted myself up. It creaked loudly, and I froze. When the guards didn't even glance my way, I put my foot up on the next one and then the next one. I dragged myself up the side of the tower until I could grab hold of the bottom rung of the ladder. The tower swayed with my weight, and I didn't wait to see if it would hold. I just had to get a bit higher and then I could launch myself over the side of the wall.

Or at least that was the plan.

The tower creaked and wobbled as I hurried up the side. Just as I reached the height I needed, something broke, and I was falling. I clutched the side of the tower as it descended toward the wall. The guards' shouts and the pounding of feet told me my time was almost up.

Falling sideways, the watchtower fell toward the wall. It was now or never. Taking a deep breath, I jumped off the side of the tower. Metal clanged and crashed as it smashed into the wall. I barely skimmed over the top of the wall, the spikes on top ripping my shirt and nicking my skin.

I hissed and then groaned as I landed on the ground with a hard thud. Metal rained down on me, a beam headed straight toward me, and I rolled. It slammed into the ground where I had been moments before. The guards were getting closer, probably checking both sides for damage. I hurried to my feet. Pain ripped through my shoulder and side, and I cried out. My hand clapped over my mouth to muffle the sound as I limped toward a grove of artificial trees.

Collapsing against the side of one, I watched as the guards searched for what caused the tower to fall. After a few minutes, they seemed to calm down and head back to their posts. Maybe they thought the wind did it or it just had gotten too old and had just fallen on its own? Didn't matter really, as long as they weren't hunting me.

I moved my arm slightly and winced. Pulling back the shredded parts of my shirt, I saw the skin ripped and bloody, but it wasn't too deep. It'd heal on its own. The nick on my side was a bit deeper, but I wouldn't need stitches. I pressed my hand to my side to stifle the bleeding. Limping more than I liked, I started through the synthetic woods and across the emerald green field. I never imagined I'd be back here, especially not in this condition. The feeling was a bit nostalgic.

The marketplace came into view. The stalls I used to buy my food from were covered. The stores closed. Without meaning to, my eyes found the butcher stall. I should tell Marsha's father. He'd want to know what happened to him. But what would I say? Marsha didn't remember me, let alone him. Probably better not to say anything. I wasn't sure he would believe me anyway.

I strolled through the market area, not in any hurry to get to where I was going. Most people here didn't have the same sense of urgency or suspicion as they did in the other areas. Most wouldn't even be bothered by a random person walking down the street in the middle of the night, though they were more likely to recognize me here than back in Middleton.

By the time I got to my old house, my limp was gone, and my arm was mostly healed. My side had stopped bleeding, but it still hadn't closed over all the way. I probably would need to feed to heal completely.

The windows were dark. Nobody was home. My stepmother and stepsisters didn't even live there anymore. They'd be further up, closer to the Core, in their brand-new house. They would have tons of servants now rather than just a handful. I always wondered where they came from. The palace? Or were they like me? Someone living out of place and forced to serve those that thought they were better? I was becoming philosophical in my non-aging years. I chuckled to myself.

A sound came from inside, and I froze. Stepping closer to the house, I peeked through the window. A figure moved. Someone was inside. But who? A curse hit my ear, and then a coppery scent filled the air. It was faint, but my senses picked it up right away. Didn't help that I felt like I was starving, probably aggravated by the blood loss.

Unlike back in the Glade, I wasn't strong enough to force myself to walk away. I couldn't even make myself stay where I was. The blood loss and lack of feeding that night had made the bloodlust impossible to deny.

Not caring who heard, I bust through the front door. It might have been unlocked, might not have, but the animal inside of me didn't care. All it wanted was the blood.

A startled sound made my eyes jerked to the sound. Missy stood in the middle of the hallway, clutching her bleeding arm to her chest. At her feet, scattered on the ground, were some of my stepmother's jewelry and some fancy silverware. When she saw me, her eyes widened, and she stepped back.

"Miss Clarabelle," Missy stuttered. "What are you doing here? Shouldn't you be in the Core?"

I grinned, and even I knew it wasn't a nice one. "I can't visit my family?" The monster in me had a sense of humor.

"Of course, you can." She bopped her head slightly. "I just meant, you know they moved. No one is here."

"You are," I reminded her, my hand trailing along the wall as I approached her. "So, I guess the trip wasn't a total waste." I flashed her a smile, and I knew by the way she gasped and put her hand to her mouth that she'd seen my fangs.

"Your eyes." She pointed a finger at my face as she backed away. "They're red."

"Are they?" I asked with a tilt of my head. "I'd never noticed." I paused in the hallway at a mirror and saw the monster looking back at me. Sharp fangs peeking over my lips, bright red eyes flashing menacingly. This is the thing I had become. The part of me that was still human screamed at me to stop, but I couldn't hear it over the pounding of Missy's blood. "You know, you really shouldn't be here either."

"I know." She cried and fell to her knees. "I'm sorry. Your mother—"

"Stepmother."

"Yes, yes." She nodded eagerly. "Your stepmother left these behind, and I thought ... I thought ..."

"You'd just help yourself?" I offered with a smirk. "You should know better than to think anything is free. Even here." I squatted down beside her, my brows furrowing in mock concern. "You hurt your hand."

Missy pushed it behind her back. "It's nothing. I'm fine."

"No, you're not." My hand shot out and grabbed her wrist pulling it toward me. "Let me see."

She whimpered in my grasp. My nostrils flared, and a low growl released from my throat. I brought her hand up to my face. It wasn't a big cut. She had probably cut it on one of the knives she was stealing. I stretched her hand out so that the blood flowed more freely, making her cry out.

My tongue darted out, sliding along her skin, curling around the blood and dragging it into my mouth. I swallowed and groaned. Divine. Animal blood really couldn't compare.

I licked her hand until the blood stopped flowing and the flesh nit back together. She watched in curious fear and, when I was done, jerked her arm back to her, her eyes scanning her newly healed hand.

"How did you ...?" she asked, staring down at her hand. "It's healed. It's completely healed."

Grinning like a wolf, I leaned in closer to her. "Do you want to know a secret?" I chuckled darkly.

She hesitated and then nodded.

I gestured for her to come forward. As she did so, I whispered in her ear, "I'm a vampire." Before she could process what I said, I struck. My fangs pierced the side of her neck. She fought against me at first, and then that euphoria I knew she would feel set in. Missy went limp against me, her hands clutching me to her.

As her blood filled my mouth, I closed my eyes. I knew that what I was doing was wrong. It was against everything I believed in, but I couldn't stop. The more I drank, the more powerful I felt. I bit her harder, making Missy moan slightly. I gripped her tighter, drinking her down even faster.

Part of me knew that I was killing her. That I'd drank too much blood. I'd have to find a way to get rid of the body. There would be questions. But I just didn't care. Was this how it was for the rest of them? So all-consuming? If so, then how the hell did they even function around humans? There had to be accidents all the time. Blood permanently in the air. I'd have to ask Asher if I ever saw him again.

Missy's hand eventually fell away, and she drooped in my arms. As my stomach filled, the hunger lessened, and somehow, I was able to pull myself away. Missy dropped to the ground in a crumpled heap. I jumped to my feet and backed away. With the bloodlust gone, my conscience came roaring back.

What had I done? I covered my mouth, my eyes burning. I stared down at her still form and shook my head over and over. I didn't do this, did I?

It felt like a dream. Like I'd been there, but I hadn't. I saw what I was doing, but I couldn't stop myself. I couldn't make myself pull away.

But that was an excuse. I knew what I was doing, I just didn't care. All I wanted was the blood. I had to have the blood.

I passed by the mirror in the hallway again and saw my face. Blood covered the bottom half, and I tried to wipe it away, but it just smeared. My pulse pounded in my ears, and the tears on my face made the blood turn a pale pink. I dragged my hair away from my face and tried to make myself look less of a wreck, but after the night I had, only a hot shower and a new change of clothes would make it better.

Unable to stand to look at myself, I spun on my heels intent on using the shower upstairs. The water had to still be on. If I were lucky, I'd even have some clothes left in my old room.

I rounded the corner and ran straight into a hard form. My eyes jumped up to the face, and I murmured, "Patrick."

Chapter 8

AS IF MY NIGHT couldn't have gotten any worse. Of all the people in all of Alban for me to run into, it had to be Patrick Blordril. The bane of my existence and cause for all my misery.

Okay, so that's a bit dramatic, but he was the cause for *most* of it.

"Patrick," I said again, breathing heavily. "What are you doing here?"

Patrick frowned. "I could ask you the same thing."

I blanched. He had a point.

"Well, I ... uh ..." I stammered trying to find a good reason to be there. When his eyes dipped down to my mouth, I remembered the blood on my face. Spinning around, I covered my lower face with my hand. "I asked you first."

Patrick sniffed and then laughed. "So, I take it we're not going to be mature about this then?"

Rage filled my chest. I jerked around and shoved a finger at his chest. "Mature about this? You're the one who did this to me. You! I have every right to react however I want."

With an impatient sigh, Patrick stared down at me like an impertinent child. "And you have every right to be upset. I'm not even mad that you ran away, even if it has caused quite a commotion with the Fold."

I snorted, rolling my eyes. "Oh, thank you, good sir, for your mercy. I am so sorry I caused you such an inconvenience when you took my life!" The sarcasm was so thick in my voice you could cut it with a knife.

Patrick's eyes grew hard, and before I could react, his hands shot out and grabbed hold of my shoulders. "You should thank me for my mercy. You have no idea what kind of mess you've made. The kind of things I've had to say and promise to keep them from hunting you down and slaughtering you and your family - just because!"

I swallowed hard at the sharpness in his voice but refused to back down. "Well, whatever it was, it couldn't have been that hard for you. After all, you are a soulless monster." I spat the words at his face, a sense of satisfaction filling me when he winced.

He released me so abruptly that I stumbled back and had to hold onto the railing to keep from tumbling over. I glared up at him, but when I saw the genuine hurt on his face, I frowned.

"Is that really what you think of me?" he asked, so softly that I almost couldn't hear him.

"Yes," I answered though as I said it, I wasn't a hundred percent sure anymore.

Patrick sighed and dragged a hand through his hair, mussing the pale locks, so they fell over his forehead. "Then I have done a piss poor job winning you over."

I barked a laugh. "You have been trying to win me over?" My brows shot up to my hairline. "Really?"

"Isn't it obvious?" Patrick asked with a sort of puppy dog look that made funny things happen to my insides.

"No, not at all." I shook my head, laughing again. "You are doing a terrible, terrible job."

"It would seem so." He gave me a pathetic smile. We were quiet for a moment, and then Patrick said, "I'm not a monster or soulless - or at least I don't think so?" His brow furrowed as he thought about it. "When Asher and I decided things needed to change, we never meant to destroy your life or anyone else's. I certainly never meant to make you one of us."

I wasn't sure what to do or say. I think Patrick was trying to apologize and the mature thing would be to accept it, but then again, he might not want me to acknowledge it. So, I settled for, "Yeah, well there are a lot of things none of us ever meant to do."

"Including eating your housekeeper?" Patrick glanced at Missy's body still laying in the middle of the hallway.

I grimaced. "Yeah, like that."

Seeing my discomfort, Patrick gestured toward the stairs. "Why don't you go clean yourself up, I'll take care of ..." We both looked back to where Missy laid.

Not one to look a gift horse in the mouth, I nodded and darted up the stairs. When I was out of Patrick's line of sight, I peeked back down the stairs, watching him as he stood there for a moment. He shifted in place, looking out the window of the house before turning down the hallway and out of view.

No longer able to spy, I went to my old bedroom in search of spare clothes. It seemed like my stepmother left a lot of things behind when they moved. Either she forgot them, or she just didn't care. I was betting the latter. When she came to my wedding, she had been bragging about all the money they had. More than likely she just bought all new stuff.

As I pulled my bedroom door open, I was relieved and a bit surprised to see my stuff where it had been when I left. I opened my closet and found an almost identical outfit to the one I was wearing. I changed out of my pants and started to pull my shirt off, but it got stuck in the dried blood.

Taking my new shirt with me, I stepped out of my room and headed to the bathroom. Turning on the facet, I hoped against hope the water was still working. When the glorious liquid poured from the pipe, I made a small shout of joy and then quickly clamped my mouth shut. I glanced toward the doorway and then back to the sink.

I grabbed a washcloth and wet it, pressing it against my side until the blood loosened up enough to pull the fabric away. Underneath the shirt, I was happy to discover, I was fully healed. Though I was upset about what happened with Missy, I couldn't dismiss the benefits of feeding on humans.

"It's miraculous, isn't it?"

I jumped in place, spinning around to see Patrick in the doorway. His eyes scanned down over my exposed skin, lingering on my chest. I grabbed the new shirt and quickly pulled it on, my face heating. "Yeah, I don't hate it."

"There are plenty of things to love about your new ... status." Patrick walked into the room fully. He reached for the washcloth, and after hesitating a moment, I let him have it. Rinsing it out, he turned to me. "May I?"

Swallowing thickly, I blushed even harder but nodded.

Patrick began to wipe away the blood on my face with surprisingly gentle hands. I wasn't sure why I was letting him do this. I should be finding a weapon to drive into his heart, or an ax to cut off his head. Not that my stepmother had any of those laying around. Bet I could find something useful back at the butcher stall.

Regardless, I shouldn't be letting him touch me, but here I was, and here he was, cleaning off the remains of Missy. I should be freaking out still about killing her, but I wasn't. I just felt embarrassed about losing control and confused about how I felt about Patrick.

"What is it?" Patrick asked, setting the rag on the sink.

"Huh?"

"You have that 'I'm thinking too hard' look on your face." He gestured to my eye region.

"I have a look like that?" I was surprised and astonished he even recognized it.

"You have quite a few looks, actually."

Shifting shyly, I asked, "Do you spend a lot of time looking at my face?"

"You're a hard one to figure out. I find studying you makes it easier. Not by much though." He offered me a small smile.

I wasn't sure if I should take it as a compliment or not. I decided not to even comment on it. No need to open that can of worms. I had enough problems.

"So, are you going to tell me why you're here?" I asked, leaning against the edge of the bathtub. Patrick opened his mouth, and I pointed a finger at him. "Don't you dare answer me with a question. I've had a long night."

Patrick smirked. "I can see that." He dipped his head down and then, with a small laugh, shook it. "I'm here for you."

Crossing one ankle over the other, I said, "Huh? Can you run that by me again?"

"You heard me." Patrick stepped up to me, pushing his way into my personal space. "Did you really think I wouldn't come after you?"

I shrugged. "Of course, I knew you would. Just didn't expect it to take you so long." Gripping the edge of the tub, I clucked my tongue. "So, what did take you so long? Are you losing your touch?"

"You just can't help yourself, can you?" Patrick asked, his lips curving up slightly.

I forced down the strange feeling it gave me and snapped, "What can I say? You bring out the worst in me."

"That's a pity." Patrick stepped even closer to me, reaching out to tuck a strand of hair behind my ear. I shifted away from his touch, not because I found it revolting but because it made the butterflies even worse. Seriously. Ever since I'd been changed, all my emotions had skyrocketed including my slight attraction to the vampire in front of me.

"So, how'd you find me, anyway?" I asked to break the tension between us. "I didn't exactly leave a note."

"I can feel you."

His words reached deep inside of me, caressed me where no one had ever touched. A shiver went through me, and it was slightly harder to breathe. It was both frightening and exhilarating.

"What do you mean, you can feel me?" I asked, my voice coming out a bit breathless. I dropped my gaze and cleared my throat, pushing the feeling away.

Patrick knelt before me, forcing me to meet his eyes. "I made you. You have my blood pumping through your veins. I will always be able to find you."

"Well, that..." My voice trailed off before a chuckle escaped my lips. "That is just creepy on all levels." When Patrick didn't respond, I asked, "Why wait until now? If you've been able to feel me this whole time, why wait until I came here?"

Standing, Patrick tucked his hands into his pockets. "Getting away from the Core isn't as easy for me as it is for you. Plus, as I said before, I've been cleaning up the mess you left behind. I just happened to be checking up on you when I felt your presence here."

"You keep saying I left a mess. What mess?" Suddenly, my heart was in my throat. "Is Marsha—"

"He's fine." Patrick quipped a bit too sharply. Someone was still jealous. For some reason now, the prospect doesn't irritate me. It amused me.

"Does he still not ...?" I asked, but the steely expression on Patrick's face told me he was done talking about Marsha.

"My turn to ask the questions." Patrick moved away from me, making it easier to breathe.

I was both thankful and disappointed. How I could be thinking of Marsha but still feel such a pull to Patrick baffled me. I couldn't care for him, could I?

"What are you doing here?" Patrick's question kept me from delving into my own emotions further.

Saving my inner turmoil for later, I thought of what to say to Patrick. Telling him that I was going to find out how many vampires there were before I reported it to the leaders of the Glade so they could destroy them all, possibly me included, well, I didn't see that going over well.

Opening my mouth to tell him some lie, Patrick stopped me.

"Don't lie to me. It won't end well for you." Patrick's tone was low and full of warning.

I swallowed the lies in my mouth and instead, for some reason that I couldn't define told him the truth.

Chapter 9

PATRICK CROSSED HIS ARMS over his chest and tapped his foot. I'd imagined he'd blow up and drag me back to the Core after hearing my plan. I didn't think he'd actually consider it.

"So, you want to know how many vampires there are?" he arched a brow. "All the vampires?"

I hesitated and then sighed. "They won't have a chance if they don't know how many vampires they are up against."

I chewed on my lower lip, contemplating the validity of my plan. Though the humans far outnumbered the vampires, they had a significant advantage over us, well, them. I hadn't been a vampire for very long, it was hard to remember that I wasn't part of the human populace anymore.

As if sensing my inner battle, Patrick asked, "Clarabelle, are you sure you want to do this?" The intensity of his eyes made me look away from him.

Licking my lips, I sighed. "I don't really have a choice now, do I? You and Asher weren't getting it done, and I'm not waiting a hundred years to slowly change things." Patrick tried to interrupt me, but I cut him off. "No. There are too many of the Fold members who want me dead. Or worse. I'll be lucky to survive the next year, let alone a century."

Patrick stayed silent for a moment before inclining his head slightly. "I understand. Perhaps Asher and I did underestimate the enemies you might make by your ... difference."

I gave him an incredulous look, making him chuckle.

"A difference I find refreshing and amusing." Patrick stepped closer to me, placing his hand on my arm. It made the hairs on my skin stand on end, and I resisted the urge to rub them away.

"Fine, sure. I'm a delight." I pulled my arm back slowly. "What about you? Are you okay with this?" I really looked at him. No shying away now. "They'll come after you. All of you."

He lifted one elegant shoulder. "I have lived long enough. If the rest of the Fold does not see reason, then I would happily forfeit my life for the humans to have a chance to start again."

I stared at him in disbelief. He would really do that? I didn't see him as the self-sacrificing type. He was more of the 'do it my way or get thrown in the dungeon' type. He'd shown me that more than once. There was also the tight feeling in my chest I got thinking about him lying dead on the ground, his head or heart missing. Just the image in my head made my eyes burn.

"What about Asher? And the others?" I asked, covering up my concern for him. "You would just let them die?"

"Would you?"

My mouth dropped open a little. "No! No. Of course, not. I expected they'd get away before this all went down."

"And go where?" Patrick caressed the side of my face. The movement was so sudden I almost thought I'd dreamed it. Why was he touching me so much? And why did I like it?

"I don't know." I squirmed in place, not liking being asked questions I didn't have the answers to. "There's got to be more beyond Alban. You said there were other

96

settlements like ours run by vampires. They could go there."

"So, you have them uproot their lives and run away to someplace that might not even accept them? Or even exist anymore?" Patrick's questions were sound, but they still pissed me off.

"What? You don't keep in contact with the other vampires?" I scoffed and rolled my eyes. "Isn't that against your ancient code or something?"

"Vampires are solitary creatures," Patrick explained with a wave of his hand. "The fact that we have come together like this is unusual for us, which is why we have so many disagreements." His lips twisted into a grimace as if thinking of something unpleasant. "Before the great war, we were either alone or possibly with a mate." The way he looked at me when he said the word mate made my whole body warm.

"That's interesting." Even I marveled at the lameness of my comment. It was interesting? That was the best I could do.

As I chastised myself, Patrick had moved even closer to me, and then, like a magnetic pull, I shifted forward as well. There was barely an inch between us now. My heart rampaged in my chest, even as I tried to figure out what was happening here.

"Why am I so drawn to you?" I blurted out, as my hand landed on his chest. My fingers curled underneath my palm, clutching his shirt in my hand.

Patrick dipped his head so that his forehead pressed against mine. "I can only assume it's because of the way you felt before I changed you." His hands came up to cup my face, his face so close to mine now that I could feel his breath on my skin.

"The way I felt before? The only thing I felt before was revulsion." I tried to make it sound insulting but couldn't think clearly enough to put the bite I needed into it.

Patrick laughed, the sound rumbling through his chest and vibrating through me. "Deny it all you want, Clarabelle, but our blood exchange cannot create the emotions, only enhance them. You cared for me before this, just as I have for you."

My eyelids fluttered uncontrollably, and I forced them to stay open to glare at him. "I did not and do not care about you."

A small, sad smile tinged his lips. "So, if I should perish during this rebellion of yours, you would not weep for me?"

"No, I wouldn't," I quickly said, but they held no truth to them. And by the way Patrick chuckled once more, he knew it.

I want to say that when his lips brushed mine, I shoved him away, but my neck had a mind of its own. It arched so that I met him, his mouth soft against mine. At first, it was a gentle rubbing of our lips, neither of us in a hurry to move it further. I, of course, had no experience in the matter, except the one time Patrick had kissed me which had turned into him marking me for conversion. I began to pull away, the reminder of it dampening my mood.

Patrick had other ideas.

Something soft and wet traced along the line of my lips, and it startled me enough that my mouth fell open, a small squeak coming out. Patrick's hands on my face drew me toward him, his tongue taking my gaping mouth as an invitation. It was a peculiar feeling, having someone else's tongue inside your mouth. Not a bad feeling but ... peculiar. Yep, that about described it.

Our bodies pressed together as I allowed him to explore my mouth. There was no biting this time, making it easier to give into the experience. For all my complaining and denying, I had to admit kissing him wasn't horrible. It made my toes curl and my stomach tingle. The longer we kissed, the warmer I became until I felt as if I might explode.

I jerked away from him, breathing heavily. This time Patrick let me, his eyes hooded. His thumb trailed along my bottom lip, a look in his eyes that I couldn't describe.

"Well," I huffed and laughed at the same time. "That was different."

"Yes." Patrick angled his head to the side. "It was."

I stared up at him for a moment and then cleared my throat and stepped away, putting some distance between us. "Uh, I should probably get going." I inched toward the doorway, my eyes on the floor.

"Clarabelle," the sound of my name on Patrick's lips did something funny to me. It made me want to kiss him once more. The feeling was so overwhelming my hands curled into fists to keep me in place.

"What?" I asked a bit harsher than I meant to.

"Aren't you forgetting something?"

My brow furrowed as I searched his face. What had I forgotten?

"You wanted to know how many vampires there are," Patrick reminded me with a smug grin on his lips. Ugh, how I wanted to smack it off and kiss it at the same time.

Get a grip, Clarabelle!

"Right," I nodded.

Patrick seemed to be laughing at me but had the decency not to comment on it. "There are thirty-two vampires including you and me. Twelve of those are Crimson Fold members. Another dozen or so are family members of the Fold, like Asher, who have been converted. The rest are mates or companions who have been converted over the years."

I nodded again, not trusting myself not to say something stupid. Turning back to the door, I made it to the stairwell before Patrick caught my wrist. I stared down at his hand before following it up to his face.

"Don't you want to know?" The look on his face was no longer amused but serious. Too bad I had no idea what he was talking about.

"Know what?"

He laced our fingers together and glanced down at the ground as he said, "If Marsha is one of the thirty-two."

His comment slammed into me like I'd been hit by my father's van. I'd been so wrapped up in Patrick and what I felt for him that I'd forgotten all about Marsha, someone I claimed to care for more than Patrick. I had a nagging feeling that might not be the case anymore.

"I assumed he was one already." I tried to cover up my mistake but for some reason didn't take my hand back.

Patrick peeked back up from our joined hands to my face. "No, he's not. Tris has decided to wait on converting him."

"Why?" I blurted out before I could think about it. "Not that I'm not happy for him, but why? Why wait?"

Sighing, Patrick brought my hand up between us. "I'd imagine because of you." He pressed his lips against the side of my hand, and for a moment, my mind went blank.

I shook my head and my hand free of his mesmerizing touch. "I don't know why. He doesn't remember me. So, what's the point?"

"But you remember him and, if you forget, were quite adamant during your trial." He seemed a bit put out about it, and I felt like I should apologize for some reason. "Now that you've done a disappearing act, she will probably be using him as collateral or maybe even bait to get you to cooperate."

I snorted. "Fat chance of that happening."

Patrick clasped his hands in front of him and shrugged. "She doesn't know that, so he will remain human for now. Though, if I were you, I wouldn't wait too much longer to start your revolution if you wish to keep it that way."

I swallowed hard and nodded. "Understood."

We moved down the stairs, neither of us speaking until we reached the bottom floor. Automatically, I searched the hallway for Missy's body and found it gone. I wanted to ask him what he'd done with it but thought it better for my own sanity not to ask.

"Are you going back to the Glade?" Patrick asked, waiting in the doorway for me.

"Yes. I was going to go to the Core, but since you answered all I needed to know, it's time for me to, as you said, 'Start a revolution.'" I ended my words with a sardonic smile.

Patrick returned my smile with one of his own and then added, "Then I would show you a quicker way back."

"A quicker way?" I asked as he led me out of my old house and toward a section of artificial trees just north of the marketplace.

He moved quickly and quietly, something I still needed to learn how to do, before stopping. There on the ground, barely visible beneath the brush, was a metal door. Pulling it open, it didn't so much as creak. Beneath it was a set of stairs that descended into dark nothingness.

"This tunnel goes underneath Alban. When you come to the junction, go left to go toward the Glade and right to go to the Core." Patrick explained in a robotic tone. So much for our moment.

I stepped toward the entrance and glanced back at him. "Thanks."

"You're most welcome." He didn't smile this time or show any emotion at all. For some reason, that bothered me even more than his usual overly charming self. As I descended into the tunnel, Patrick's face haunted me, and I answered the question he had asked me truthfully.

Yes, I'd miss him if he died. More than I could measure.

Chapter 10

PATRICK'S INSTRUCTIONS HAD BEEN dead on, and the tunnel hadn't been as dark as I thought it had been. Super senses to the rescue.

When I found the end of the tunnel, I was relieved to see it came out in the Glade, surprisingly, well, not really, next to the graveyard. Probably didn't think too many people would come looking around here.

The sky had lightened, the red and yellow colors signaling sunrise. I'd been gone all night. Thankfully, my stomach was full because the Glade was in full swing. The life of a farmer at its best.

Instead of heading for my shack, I went straight to my father's house. As I walked by, the workers' heads popped up. At first, confusion colored their faces, then surprise. Eventually, there were whispers. Not to me though. I could hear them clear as day, I just chose to ignore them.

Let them say what they wanted. This wasn't about me anymore.

I stomped up the stairs of our porch, one of the only houses with one. A benefit of being the overseers, one of the only ones. I didn't bother to knock, I shoved the door open.

It wasn't surprising to see him sitting at our table with the others who helped run the Glade. They always had a meeting at dawn. No one wanted to spend all night arguing over issues, not that I would want to this early either.

When I busted in, all five heads - including my father's - jerked up. Their expressions matched that of the villagers outside, a mixture of surprise and confusion. Except for my father. Well, he was surprised but not for the same reasons as them.

"Clarabelle!" My father stood up, glancing at the other leaders, who turned to him for an explanation. "I didn't know you were coming."

Stepping further into the room, I closed the door behind me. "I found out what I needed to."

I looked at the other four, one for each part of the Glade. I didn't know any of them, not personally. I'd seen them here in our home every day until we moved to the Inner Circle. They watched me grow up. I was hoping those factors would help them not freak out about what I was about to tell them.

"Hello." I gave a slight wave. "I didn't mean to interrupt your meeting, but as you can see, I'm not exactly supposed to be here." I smiled awkwardly.

Mara, an older woman with a kind face who had always made sure to check on me after my mother passed, was the first to come forward. "Clara." Her soft voice caused a nostalgia to fill me. "It's good to see you." She hugged me tightly, and I froze.

I could hear her blood pumping through her veins. Even though I'd already eaten, my fangs ached. I forced myself to hug her back before getting away from her. Thankfully, no one else tried to hug me. I didn't think I could handle it.

"Not that it's not good to see you," Dale, a balding man who oversaw the herders, said, "but what are you doing here? Shouldn't you be up there?" He pointed in the direction of the Core. "You know, being married and such."

I nodded. "Yes, I probably should be." I turned from him and met my father's worried gaze. "Except I can't. During my time in the Core, I've learned about some disturbing things, especially about our esteemed leaders."

They shifted uncomfortably and murmured to themselves, but I didn't stop to let them dismiss me. Moving closer, I stayed at one end of the table, my fingers splayed out on the wooden surface.

"Some of you might not remember how Alban came to be." I glanced around the table as I spoke, taking in their expressions. "Some of you probably have a watered-down version of it like my father, but I'm here to tell you that everything you know, everything you think you knew about our leaders, is a lie."

This time they didn't keep their voices down when they spoke their doubt. I kept my eyes on my father, watching him for some kind of warning, but he only nodded his head. This was the time. It was now or never.

Not surprisingly, Dale was the first to speak out. "I don't mean to be rude, but don't you think you are being a bit dramatic? You're only seventeen. You're too young to understand the way the world works." He looked around the table and chuckled, causing the others except my father and Mara to laugh too. "Maybe you should be asking your husband about this."

The mention of Patrick and that I was too young, too naive to know what I was talking about pissed me off beyond measure. In my mind, I grabbed Dale by the throat and ripped his spine out from his flesh. In reality, I took a deep breath and stared hard at the table.

"Dale," I started, happy that my voice didn't shake with my anger. "Not to be rude," I parroted his condescending words back at him, "but you don't know what the hell you are talking about." Dale tried to argue with me, but I didn't give him a chance. "We sit out here so far from the Core that we don't know what is really going on in our world."

My eyes snapped to Mara. "For example, did you know there are other settlements like ours? Set up exactly like this. Farmers on the outside, industrial workers in the middle, and the privileged, the soft hands, closest to the leaders." I spat the word as it curdled in my mouth. "Have you ever wondered why that is? Why we barely get by while they get fed until their clothes hardly fit?" They were quiet as if really thinking about what I was saying. My impatience made me ask again, "Well, have you?"

This time it was Mara who answered me back. "Clara, I think I speak for most of us when I say" - she nodded to the others - "we're doing what we must to survive."

The laugh that came out of me wasn't pleasant. "You call this surviving? We have how many deaths a month? If not from starvation, then from infection or sickness? I cut my face, and they healed it within a matter of seconds." I snapped, my head swiveling between them making sure I caught all their gazes. "How is that fair?"

There was a mumbled answer from a small thin man. Nex, I believed it was.

"What was that?" I asked, arching my ear to hear him. He had said it too low for even my vampire hearing to pick up.

Clearing his throat, Nex met my eyes. "I said, isn't that life though? It's never fair."

"Right." Dale gestured to Nex. "And besides, what do you expect us to do? Rise up and revolt? What would that accomplish? We don't have weapons to fight with. Those blasters guarding the entrance to the Glade would stop us before we got anywhere.”

There was a collective agreement that made Dale cross his arms with a smug look on his face. He turned to my father before I could counter him. “Richard, I respect you and your authority, but I’m sorry, I can’t put my family or our people at risk because of your daughter’s flights of fancy.”

Flights of fancy? Flights of fancy! My teeth ground together, and I knew I was close to losing my grip on my temper. Ripping Dale’s throat out was looking better and better by the minute.

“Dale,” my father said, finally stepping in. “Please, just listen to her.”

“I am,” Dale snapped. “Are you? This is a bunch of crap. We don’t need another uprising. Don’t you remember the last one?” He raised a brow, making my father frown.

“This is not like it was back then. This isn’t just the poor wanting what the rich have,” my father tried to reassure him.

“Isn’t it?” Dale scoffed. “Because that’s what it sounds like to me.” His eyes landed on me and glowered. “You know what happens when we get too greedy.”

This was getting ridiculous. I had tried to ease them into this. To make them see how wrong the way we were set up was without bringing the whole vampire thing up yet. Apparently, that wasn't working. I didn't know much about the last uprising. It was before my time, but this wasn't anything like then. Back then, they had a bunch of idiots thinking they could beat the system with pitchforks and their righteousness.

I exchanged a look with my father, and I could tell he wasn't happy about what I was about to do, but we both knew it was the only way to get them to listen. Before I could make my grand reveal, Dale pushed away from the table and started for the door.

"I'm not going to sit here and listen to this nonsense. I have work to do." He stopped and pointed back at the table. "And I suggest the rest of you get back to work as well before she drags us all down to an early grave."

Enough was enough. As Dale turned back around, I moved. In what must have looked like a blur to Dale, I appeared in front of him, making him back up, his eyes wide and his mouth agape.

"How ... how did you do that?" He glanced behind him and back to me. The others at the table sans my father was just as astonished.

"Like I was trying to tell you," I grinned, flashing my fangs. "You don't know what the hell you are talking about."

Dale backed away from me in a hurry, scurrying back to the table. I sauntered back to them, making sure to put my fangs away as I approached them. All except my father stared at me in wonder and fear.

Good. Hopefully, they would listen now.

"Mara," I began and hated that she flinched away from me. "You know me, would I ever hurt someone on purpose?"

"N … no. Never." She shook her head.

"Do you think I was hiding this?" I gestured to myself. "Hiding for the last seventeen years? Do you?" I glared at them, daring them to say something stupid. "This was done to me by the Crimson Fold, and they have done this to countless others. How do you think Patrick Blordril looks the same as his predecessor, and him the one that came before? I'll give you a hint. He's the same person."

Realization began to fill their faces. It wasn't hard to figure out if you really thought about it. It only took someone putting the thought in their minds. I was just happy I finally had them listening. Now, if I could just bring it home.

"The election they have every year?" I continued, scanning the table. "They aren't held to gift us with a new life. The election is to fill their palace with workers who will keep quiet and to make brainless meat sacks to feed on. They have a whole dungeon full of them." The image of Tillie sitting on her cot with a blank look on her face filled my mind. The very thought of it made my throat clot with emotion. "They have been playing us this whole time, using us to give them a never-ending food supply."

There was silence in the room, and then all at once, they started talking over each other. There was a mixture of questions and fears. One of the men, a large man with a mean look in his eye, wanted to kill me right there.

"We can't do that!" Mara argued with him. "She's trying to help us. Why would we kill someone who might be our only chance at survival?"

"But she's one of them," he growled, his teeth gnashing at me. "How do we know this isn't some trick? Maybe the others are waiting for us to come storming in so they can do exactly what she said."

I shook my head, impatience in my voice. "That would be pointless. Especially since they don't know I'm here. They want me dead more than you right now."

"Why?" Dale glared. "Why do they want you dead?"

I glowered at him. "The same reason you do. I'm different."

"What exactly are you?" Nex asked, his voice shaking. "What kind of monster are we dealing with?"

I flashed a fang with an unhappy grin. "I'm a vampire, and we're going to take back Alban."

Chapter 11

"WELL, THAT WENT WELL." My father plopped back down in his seat as soon as the other leaders left. I couldn't say that he wasn't right.

After my big reveal, the leaders couldn't get out of there fast enough. We'd decided to keep things hush-hush until we could reconvene and decide on our next move. I just hoped they kept their word. It would suck to wind up on the receiving end of an angry mob.

"Do you think I'm doing the right thing?" I asked him, taking a seat next to him. "Should I have even told them about me being a vampire?"

My father raised his brow. "Are you worried about what they might do to you?" I nodded. Placing his hand on top of mine, he gave me a sympathetic look. "I won't let anything happen to you, I promise."

I smiled gently at him, though I was pretty sure he was wrong. He couldn't save me. If anything, I'd be lucky to protect myself and any of my friends still in the Core.

"So, what now?" I asked after a moment, breaking up the moment. "I told the leaders, and now they're believers, but what next? I line up the rest of the Glade to see the big bad vampire?" Sarcasm dripped from my voice in waves.

My father opened his mouth and then closed it before opening it again. "No, that's probably not a good idea. The fewer people who know about you, the better. If we can get them to follow us just based on what you have told us, I think it'd be best to leave out what you are."

"Yeah." I let out a heavy breath. "That'd be good."

He laced his fingers in front of him on the table. "There's something I have to ask you though."

"What is it?" I leaned my elbows on the table.

"Dale had a good point." He sighed and shook his head. "If we even get the people to rally, how are we going to get into the

Core or even the other sections to tell them about it?" He made a noise in the back of his throat. "I mean, I can get in during deliveries, but I can't take that many people. Not enough to do any good."

"Well," I said with a frown, my brows scrunched together, "if you could pass the information along on your deliveries, that would take care of that part."

"Okay." He moved his head to the side and then looked back at me. "What about getting past the guards?"

I thought about it for a moment, and then I had a duh moment. I knew a way to get in and out of the Core and any other section without detection, the way I'd just used not over an hour ago.

"There's a tunnel," I began, staring down at my hands. Even as I was saying it, I felt guilty. Patrick had told me about the tunnel in confidence, and here I was turning around and giving the information over to those who would hurt him.

"A tunnel?"

I cleared my throat and rubbed my nose, like that would make my guilt go away. "It goes underneath all of Alban. Probably how the Fold gets around without being seen."

"How did we not know about this?" my father scoffed, his fingers playing with the stubble on his chin.

"The entrance is hidden by the graveyard, or at least one of them is. There's another north of the marketplace in the Inner Circle. I'd imagine there is another one in Middleton. And while I don't know where it is, I know there's one in the Core."

"Well, that's ..." He trailed off with a slight chuckle. "Convenient."

"Yeah."

"How did you find out about it?" He looked at me expectantly, and I couldn't find the words.

I couldn't tell him that Patrick told me. I didn't know why. Okay, that was a lie. I understood why. I didn't want Patrick to be on their radar. I wanted to keep him out of it, as if somehow I could save him by not talking about him. Not that I was sure it would help. Still, I had to try.

"In a book," I said finally. "They have a lot of books in the Core. Dang vampires document everything." I sniffed and smiled, the words tasted like acid in my mouth.

"Huh." That's all my father had to say about it. I couldn't tell if he believed me or not, but if he didn't, he wasn't saying so.

Which was fine by me. I had enough to deal with.

A wave of exhaustion fell over me at that. Not surprising, since I'd been up all night and most of the morning. I needed to sleep soon. I pushed up from the table and started for the door.

"Where are you going?" my father asked, standing as well.

"I need to get some sleep," I explained. "I'll be in the shack." I reached for the door handle and then stopped, my hand dropping. "Uh, actually that might not be a good idea. Everyone saw me come up here. If I went back to the shack, there might be questions."

"I guess you're right." He hummed and then came around the table to stand beside me. "I guess that just means you'll have to stay here."

I looked at him wryly. "Are you sure?"

"Of course." He placed his hand on my shoulder. "You're my daughter. Plus, your room is just sitting there, not being used. Might as well use it while you can."

I swallowed back my gratitude and nodded. I didn't want to think about what he meant by those words. It could have meant I'd be living again in the Core or, the worst-case scenario, I would be dead. Either way, I didn't want to think about it.

My room looked exactly how I left it. To one side of the room sat a low cot with a threadbare sheet and a wooden box at the end of the bed. I didn't have many clothes, not like back at the Core where they had a vast wardrobe and too many choices. Just out of curiosity, I moved over to the box and popped the top.

I didn't know what I expected to find. I'd moved all my stuff except for the furniture to my stepmother's house. There was a button and a handful of drawings I'd made as a child, except for one which I recognized as a doodle I'd done last year.

Smirking, I looked down at my crappy picture of what I thought was a girl riding a horse. As I laid down on the bed, I realized it looked more like a donkey than a horse. It was funny that when I had drawn this picture, I'd been more worried about getting stuck late for a meeting than starting a revolt.

I didn't know when I drifted off to sleep, but I was jolted awake by the feeling of someone watching me. I shot up in bed, my hand still clutching the picture from the box. The sun had set, and the moon sat high in the sky, the light pouring through my little window. My father had probably gone to sleep already.

I scanned the room, but there was no one there. Still, the nagging feeling of someone watching me didn't go away. Slipping out of bed, I moved across the room and then spun in place. My brow furrowed, I tried to figure out what had woken me up.

Turning to the door, I reached for the doorknob. There it was. The feeling. Before I could overthink about it, I twisted the handle and whipped the door open. There, standing on the other side, was Patrick in all his vampiric splendor.

"What, do you just have a never-ending supply of white suits?" I leaned against the doorway looking him over like he wasn't making my insides jump all over the place.

Glancing down at himself, he frowned before meeting my eyes. "I happen to like these suits. They fit well."

"But they make you look like an albino." I moved out of the doorway and gestured for him to come in. I didn't bother with stupid questions, like how he found me, or how he got in there. He's a vampire. Locks really didn't have any meaning to super strength.

"I'm not sure what you mean, but alright. I'll make a note of it." He tucked his hands

122

into his pockets and looked so sincere that I had to pick on him.

"You'll make a note of it?" I laughed and sat on my bed. "Just like that? Why are you being so accommodating?"

"Well," Patrick murmured as he strolled across the room, stopping at the foot of the bed, his eyes scanning the paltry surroundings. "You're my wife. I would want to make sure you are pleased with my appearance."

I blanched. "Your ... your wife?"

Patrick arched a brow. "Did you forget? Your friends and family gathered. You walked down the aisle. We said some words."

"Oh, I remember." I held my hand up to stop him from going further. "I just didn't expect you to think it meant anything."

"It didn't to you?" He tilted his head to the side ever so slightly, confusion covering his face. "I thought those kinds of things were important to your kind."

"Well, technically, I'm more your kind now." I huffed and adjusted on the bed. "But most of us, yes, do take marriage seriously, but seeing as it was a forced arrangement, I didn't think you were going to hold me to it." I stared up at him expectantly, and then a horrible thought crossed my mind. "You aren't, are you?"

Patrick pressed his lips into a thin line as he made a disgusted sound. "Don't look at me that way, Clarabelle. I might be a vampire, but I'm no monster. I am not here to take you against your will. I am a gentleman."

I couldn't help but snort. "Like that's ever stopped you before."

His pale eyes narrowed, and I wished I hadn't said anything. "It was either change you or kill you and your family. Which would you have preferred?"

I couldn't hold his stare and dropped my eyes to the floor. Shame filled me.

"As I thought." Patrick shifted, and then the bed dipped beside me. "Stop trying to make me the villain in this. Haven't I proven to you yet that I'm on your side?"

"Yes," I said lowly, emotion clogging my throat. Turning my head away from him, I coughed a few times to clear it. Using a finger, I brushed the tear that tried to fall away before he could see it. "So, if you're not here to take advantage of me, then what are you doing here?"

A hand took hold of my chin and turned my face to him. He frowned at me as his thumb traced underneath my eyes where

I'd wiped away my tear. My lips trembled beneath his gaze, the brave face I'd been forcing to the front starting to weaken.

"You needn't be so strong in front of me, Clarabelle." His words were low and did nothing to stop me from breaking.

"I have to be brave, or I'll fall apart." My voice broke, and I couldn't stop the tears from falling. It was all just too much for me. The marriage, the change, losing Marsha, and now saving everyone in Alban from the very thing I'd become. I was surprised I'd held on this long under all that crushing weight on my shoulders.

"It's alright if you fall," Patrick reassured me, his thumb brushing along the bottom of my lip. "Because I will always be there to catch you." He pressed his mouth against mine, and this time, I didn't hesitate. I pushed into him hard, a sort of desperation filling me and only his touch would calm it.

Patrick stroked my face and pulled back from me to whisper sweet nothings in my ear before taking my mouth once more. This continued until I wasn't feeling like my heart was going to explode out of my chest and my tears had dried.

Sniffling, I withdrew from him and started trying to make up some excuse for letting him kiss me, but before it could leave my mouth, my bedroom door opened.

"Clara, I heard something and wanted to see if you were alright." My father froze in the doorway, his mouth dropped as he took in the scene before him. When his eyes fell on Patrick, his face scrunched up, his teeth gnashing. "What the hell is he doing here?"

Chapter 12

I JUMPED TO MY feet, getting some distance between Patrick and myself as I headed over to my raging father. Patrick didn't so much as flinch and seemed far too at ease for my comfort.

"Oh, hey, Father. I'm fine. That sound was just Patrick and me having a disagreement." I tried to block my father's view of Patrick but wasn't having much luck.

"You mean a disagreement involving you leading a revolt to destroy him and his twisted group?" he snarled over my shoulder, trying to push his way past me.

I put a hand up and used my vampiric strength to keep him in place. He stared down at me in surprise. "Please, stop for a moment. I know what this looks like, but you have to understand, Patrick is one of the Fold who shares our goals."

"It's true, Mr. Feldman." Patrick came up behind me, his hand settling on my shoulder. My father's eyes glared at that hand, but Patrick didn't move it away. Stubborn men.

"I hardly find your words reassuring," my father snapped and then turned on his heels, stomping back into the living area. Casting a warning look over my shoulder, I hurried after him, not caring if Patrick followed or not.

"Father," I sighed, stopping next to him, "just let me explain."

"I don't need to hear any explanation. It's obvious what's going on here." He growled as he started opening and shutting cabinets.

"What are you looking for?" I asked, trying to appease him somehow. Patrick entered the room and made the sound decision to stand as far away from my rampaging father as possible. Smart man.

"I'm just looking for a ..." His voice trailed off as he opened another cupboard before grabbing something out and slamming it shut. "A cup." He lifted it in the air to show me before turning to the beat-up refrigerator. It buzzed with life which was unusual for this time of year. Electricity wasn't that common in the Glade, we had to use a lot of our perishables before they went bad. My father pulled a pitcher of some dark brown liquid out and filled his cup before putting it back.

Taking the chance to talk while he drank deeply from his cup, I moved even closer. "I'm sure you're confused and upset, but I want you to know that Patrick really is on our side."

The cup slammed against the counter making me wince, and my father stared at me hard. "You want me to believe this monster. This man who promised me he'd love and cherish you for the rest of your life isn't the one who changed you to be just like him?"

I paled and quickly said, "No, he's not. Patrick didn't—"

"Clarabelle." Patrick's voice interrupted me. I glanced back at him, and he gave me a reassuring look. "It's alright." To my father, he said, "It was me who changed her. I was given a choice by the other Crimson Fold members, change her or kill her. I chose the prior and prayed she wouldn't hate me for it later."

My father gaped at him as I did, but Patrick continued as if we weren't looking at him like a crazy person.

"I care deeply for your daughter, Mr. Feldman." Patrick tucked his hands into his pockets and dipped his head. "And while I admit it is my fault she was chosen in the first place, I can't say I regret it. Your daughter is an amazing woman, someone I would be proud to call my wife if she ever gave me the chance." This time, his eyes moved to me, the genuine emotion there making my heart jump into my throat.

"Fine." My father snapped, and I turned back to him. "So, you're sorry. You had a hard decision, and you chose to save her. Fine. I can accept that." He glanced at me with a sad smile. "I can't say I wouldn't have done the same if I was in his position. However ..."

His smile dropped as his eyes swiveled back to Patrick. "What I can't forgive is how you could let this happen in the first place? How could you let it get this bad for so long? You have all the power, and we have nothing, no way to know what is going on, save for my daughter, who had to be smuggled out just to let everyone know the truth."

"I know." Patrick nodded. "And I have no excuse but my own cowardice. I might be the oldest of my kind, but it wasn't until recently that I have come to appreciate the life around me. It was actually Asher" - Patrick smiled at me, and I couldn't help but grin back - "that made me see what they, what we were doing was wrong. But you have to understand." Patrick stepped closer, his hands up in a harmless manner. "I might be their leader, but they are still vampires. One wrong word and the entirety of them would fall upon me, and then no one would be there to speak for your kind. Finding Clarabelle was a blessing in that way."

His hand slid into mine, and I didn't pull away. I realized the profoundness of letting him hold my hand in front of my father. It said I was standing by his side, and I couldn't say that I didn't like it.

"So, what's your plan?" my father said after a moment of processing Patrick's words. "How are you going to make sure that my daughter survives this?" He nodded towards us, clearly avoiding looking where our hands were. "She's already lit a fire in the people here, and it's too late to go back. If they make for the

Core, how will you make sure those who don't deserve to die get out alive?"

Patrick stiffened at his words before a mask of stone covered his face. "I will do what I have to in order to keep those I love safe."

Love? My eyes widened, and my mouth dropped open. I tried to mentally make Patrick look at me, but he kept his eyes forward on my father. How could he drop something that huge on me without acknowledging me at all?

My father shifted uncomfortably, not caring for his words, but not saying anything about it. "I'm happy to hear it, but that doesn't explain what you are doing in my house uninvited in the middle of the night."

"That's my fault." I stepped in front of Patrick before he could answer. "I asked him to come so we could talk."

Raising a brow, my father surveyed me curiously. "Talk about what?"

I wasn't fast enough to give an excuse before Patrick answered for me. "About Marsha." I spun around so fast it made me dizzy. "I was here to talk to her about helping Marsha."

"You were?" I asked and then when Patrick stared at me meaningfully, I quickly nodded. "Right, right. Marsha needs our help." I turned back to my father, a sad expression on my face. "It's really horrible what they did to him. He doesn't remember anything. The election, anything. He's pretty much this woman, Tris', toy." Just talking about it made anger rise in me.

My father seemed startled by my admission and took another drink from his cup. The more I stared at it, the more I had a feeling it wasn't something he would regularly drink. Alcohol, most likely. A part of me was ashamed. Had I really reduced my father to this? Drinking his problems away?

Choosing to ignore his new vice the way he had so quickly overlooked how close Patrick and I were in front of him, I worked on reassuring him the only way I could. Placing my hands on his shoulders, I gave them a squeeze. "Everything will be alright. Just wait. You'll see."

Snorting, my father dragged me into a tight hug. "I hope you're right. For the sake of us all, I hope you are right."

I let him hug me for as long as he wanted. I didn't know when we'd have the chance again. If it bothered Patrick, he didn't say so, and I didn't care. He might not remember much of his family, but my father was the only thing I had left, and I wasn't going to give him up so quickly.

After my father released me, he told us good night and for Patrick to lock up behind him when he left. Alone once more, I stared off where my father had disappeared worry filling me. Patrick had to call my name more than once to get me to look at him.

"Hm?"

"It will be alright, Clarabelle." His tone was so sure, so confident. I had a tough time not believing him, even though I had said the same thing to my father and knew that half of it had been a lie.

Not wanting to linger on it any longer, I asked, "Did you mean it?"

"Mean what?"

I walked over to Patrick and placed my hand on his arm, staring up at him beneath my lashes. "About saving Marsha. Did you mean it?"

Patrick smiled softly. "I never say something I don't mean."

"Can you really do it?" I asked, trying to ignore the way his hand settled on my hip so naturally. "Give him his memories back?"

Patrick's fingers slid underneath the hem of my shirt and drew lazy circles on my skin, making my head feel funny. "I can't promise anything. I've restored memories on a smaller scale but nothing like they did to him." He paused for a moment, and I tipped my head back completely to meet his gaze. "Would it make you happy? If I did this?"

I chewed on the inside of my cheek and thought about what he was asking. If he could return Marsha's memories, then we had a chance to be together. However, things had changed since his memories had been taken. We weren't the same two kids promising to go on a date in an impossible situation. Heck, I wasn't even human anymore. I wasn't even sure if he'd still want to be my friend, let alone anything else.

There was also the matter of Patrick. How I felt about him had changed so significantly over the last two days, I couldn't just ignore it. Also, he just told my father he loved me! How could I just throw Marsha in his face after that? I couldn't ... but I also couldn't leave Marsha to rot with that piece of trash, Tris.

Taking a deep breath, I arched up on my tip toes and pressed my lips to Patrick's. It was a brief kiss but the first I'd ever initiated, which made it even more nerve-racking. Dropping back on my heels, I breathed out my answer, "Yes, that would make me happy."

Patrick's hands curled tightly against my hips as he pressed me firmly against him. "Then I will do everything in my power to make it so."

He kissed me again after that, this time fiercer as if he were trying to ingrain himself into my memory. Like he needed to try. He was the only person I'd ever kissed, and as I laid in my bed after he'd gone, I had a feeling he'd be the last one I'd ever kiss as well.

We'd agreed to meet later that day in the tunnels where he would take me to Marsha, and we'd attempt to bring him back. I had been sad to see him go, and almost asked him to stay, but knew what that would imply, and I wasn't quite ready for that step yet. If I'd ever be.

"Just get through this alive. Then you can worry about romance," I told myself, trying to lull myself to sleep, but my mind was too busy. It wasn't until the light touched the sky that I finally fell asleep. This time, when I closed my eyes, the last thing I thought about was a pair of pale eyes and a small smile that made my heart flutter.

Oh, was I in trouble.

Chapter 13

I TOSSED AND TURNED all morning. By the time I got up, I felt as if I hadn't slept a wink. Not conducive for a rescue mission.

Cleaning up the best I could, I left my room to find my father and the leaders sitting at our kitchen table. When the floorboards creaked beneath my feet signaling my arrival, all five heads looked up. Only two of the three didn't look at me with some form of disdain or fear. I guess I should have expected it.

"Hey." I gave a small wave which only my father and Mara returned with a nod. I met my father's eyes and said, "I'm going to go do that thing we talked about last night."

"Alright, be safe," he said, dismissing me without another word. I wasn't sure what that was all about, but I had a feeling it had to do with the unsettling atmosphere in the room.

"What thing?" Dale asked, suspicion in his voice. He looked to my father and then to me, his eyes hard.

My father answered before I could say something sarcastic. "Nothing you need to worry about. Now, Clarabelle said the tunnel entrance was over here." He pointed to a worn-out paper on the table in front of him. One look told me it was a map of Alban. Looked like they were planning their attack. No wonder they didn't want me around.

"How do we know this isn't some trick?" the bald man, I still didn't know's name, snarled at me as if it were me who was the enemy. "How do we know that there won't be Core soldiers waiting for us on the other side?"

"Quell ..." my father started, but I cut him off.

"You don't." I quipped before my father could try and defend me again. No good was going to come out of letting him fight my battles. "But you have to trust that I want what is best for you and the rest of Alban. Otherwise, why would I have brought this to you?"

Quell gestured violently at me. "I don't know. Maybe this is some twisted game you monsters play to get your rocks off. You said they were crazy. How do we know this isn't just another one of their past-times? Pick off the weak and disloyal every century or so?"

Honestly, it was a good idea. If I'd been as cruel and vicious as the Crimson Fold, I'd have probably done that very thing. Kill any kind of rebellion before it could start. However, I wasn't that type of person or, well, vampire. But, I didn't see how I'd be able to convince someone so bound and determined to condemn me for others like me.

"For all my word is worth, I can assure you it's not." I sighed and glanced at Mara, her expression full of concern. "No one knows you are coming. You can strike fast and hard. There is a total of thirty-two vampires, including myself."

"Good, then we can start with you." Quell jumped at me before anyone could do anything, but I was faster.

I stepped to the side and grabbed his arm, using his forward momentum to knock him to the ground. I pulled his arm tight behind his back until he cried out in pain.

"You can't use brute force to kill me," I growled into his ear, pushing on his arm just a bit more before letting him go. Turning back to the table, I scanned my eyes over the fearful faces. "Vampires aren't just ageless. They're fast and strong. They can hear you before you can even think about sneaking up on them."

"So, what can we do?" Mara asked, her eyes going to Quell where he stumbled to his feet. "How can we possibly win?"

I offered her a small smile. "By being smarter." To the rest of the table, I said, "Attack in numbers, never go at it alone or they will use their powers of compulsion against you. And aim for the head." I slashed my hand out to where Quell came up behind me, causing him to stop in his tracks. "And the heart." I pointed a finger at Quell's heart. "Any kind of weapon will do. If you cut off the head or destroy the heart, they won't be able to heal."

"Why are you doing this?" Nex asked, a nervous tick in his cheek. "I mean, you're one of them now. Aren't you afraid you'll get brought down with them?"

I shrugged. "I don't want to die. I also didn't want to be changed into this, but there's nothing I can do about it but make sure no one else is turned into a monster."

And escape while I still could, though that part I kept to myself.

"You better go." My father gave me a meaningful look, reminding me that Patrick was waiting for me.

With a soft smile and a nod, I turned to the door. I gave Quell a warning look before pushing past him, making sure to bump my shoulder against his on the way. Childish? Sure, but the guy had just tried to kill me. I was allowed a little bit of childishness for that. After all, my days of being a child were over. It was time to figure out the rest of my existence, well, if I lasted that long.

When I stepped outside the house, the smell of burning wood hit my nose. My eyes instantly searched out the fire and found a group of teens and young adults hanging around a giant bonfire. Their laughter wafted through the air, and a sense of longing filled me. I'd never get to be one of them again. The thought hurt me more than any words Quell or the others could have said to me. I knew my place now, and it wasn't with them.

I moved down the path toward the graveyard, my eyes down on the ground. So much had happened over the past few months, it was hard to believe I was still the same person. Well, minus the vampire part. I wondered what the next few months or even years would bring. Would I still be here? Would Alban still be here? Or would everything burn to ash?

As I stepped into the bundle of trees near the graveyard, a branch cracking caused all my questions to evaporate. I tensed, searching the area, my eyes perked for an attack. Another crack of wood and I spun around, fangs bared.

Patrick stood behind me, an amused expression on his face, his hands up in the air. "Easy now."

Relaxing, I frowned. "Don't do that. I'm already jumpy as it is."

Coming out of the tree line, Patrick walked over to me. "Why? Are you nervous?"

"No." I shook my head. "Just too many things going on in my head right now." I sighed and stared down at the ground. "My father and the other leaders were at the house when I got up and let's just say the encounter was not pleasant."

"I see." Patrick hummed and then placed a hand on my lower back urging me forward. "Well, it is almost over. Then you won't have to worry about them anymore." He stopped us by the entrance to the tunnel. "For tonight, just worry about helping Marsha. The rest will follow suit."

I stared up at him, not quite knowing what to make of him. "Why are you doing this? You hate Marsha. I'd think you'd more likely want him to die with the rest of them, not save him."

Patrick placed his hands on either side of my arms and rubbed them up and down. The feeling that came from it was more than just nice, and I had to force myself not to lean into his touch. "I told you before, I'm your husband. I want to do what will make you happy, and if that means helping the boy, then I will do so."

I smiled slightly at his reference to Marsha. At least some things hadn't changed. He and Marsha had never seen eye-to-eye, not just because of the vampire thing, but because they both thought they had some claim to me. Not that I'd ever discouraged either one. It was still funny that Patrick was doing anything for Marsha at all. That left the fact that if he wasn't doing it out of the goodness of his heart, that meant he was doing it for me, and I didn't know I felt about that.

Shifting out of his grasp, I busied myself with opening the tunnel. Patrick followed me down the stairs, closing the door behind us. If we'd been human, we'd have been in complete darkness, but instead, the inside was a mixture of grays.

We walked for a while, neither of us bothering to use our super speed to get to the Core faster. It was a comfortable walk, no words were needed between us, which I think bothered me even more than if it had been awkward.

Needing to break the silence, I asked, "What you said last night to my father about you know ...?" I trailed off, tucking my hair behind my ear and ducking my head. I couldn't bring myself to say the actual words. It would make it too real.

"About what?" Patrick asked, his voice closer to me than it had been before, making me jump slightly.

Thankfully, it was dark enough that he couldn't see the blush on my face. Or at least, I hoped not. I knew he could see my hands wringing in front of me as I tried to figure out how to ask my question without actually saying it. Forcing myself to stop fidgeting, I crossed my arms tightly over my chest.

"When you said that you ... you know ... about me." I chewed on my bottom lip and kept my eyes down, not daring to meet his gaze.

"You mean when I said that I loved you?" His shoulder brushed mine, and I glanced up. A small smile played on his lips, and I knew he was laughing at my discomfort.

A bit breathless, I murmured, "Yeah, that."

"Didn't I say before that I never say anything I don't mean?" he raised a brow. "It includes that as well."

I glanced away from the intensity of his gaze, not able to stop the grin that spread across my lips. "Oh."

Yeah, I'm an articulate one.

There wasn't much else to say after that. I wasn't about to declare my love for him since I was still getting used to the idea of liking the guy. Plus, there's the whole plotting to destroy his people, maybe even him and myself included. That kind of put a damper on the whole love confessions.

Suddenly, I was pressed up against the wall of the tunnel, Patrick's breath hot against my skin. I wiggled against him, not really struggling, just trying to find a more comfortable position.

"What was that for?" I asked, looking up into his eyes and trying not to focus on how good he felt against me. How was it possible that we fit together so right? Like we were two puzzle pieces meant to be together? And when did I get so whimsical?

"To stop you from thinking so much," he answered, brushing his nose against mine, his lips so close to mine I thought he would kiss me.

I anticipated it and dared to admit I wanted it. I'd never wanted anything more than Patrick's lips against mine. So, when he shifted away from me, and I moved with him, I felt like a splash of freezing water had landed on me. The chuckle that followed only irritated me more.

Shoving away from him, I stomped down the tunnel. Stupid vampires. Stupid emotions. Who had time for romance? I had a world to save.

Chapter 14

ABOUT THE TIME WE exited the tunnel, my nerves kicked in. I'd just escaped the Core, and here I was going back? What was I, crazy?

No, just too selfless. I couldn't leave Marsha in here the way he was without trying to help him. After all, it was partly my fault they punished him. Especially because it was my fault they punished him the way they did. No one was more vindictive than a jealous woman.

"Do you want to go back?" Patrick asked as he helped me up the stairs. I hated that he could read me so well now. I wanted to freak out all on my own without someone there to tell me it will be all right. At the same time, I liked that he could anticipate my needs.

What could I say? I was a complicated mess.

"No." I shook my head, a determination filling me. "I can't. I'd feel like a coward if I didn't at least try."

"No one would know. Not even Marsha," Patrick reminded me with a small squeeze of my hand.

"Yeah." I dipped my head down to our adjoined hands and then back up to his face. "But I would, and that's not something I can live with."

Patrick inclined his head. "Understood."

He led me away from the door which had opened into a part of the garden I'd never seen. Many hedges were surrounding it, and when the door shut, vines covered the top, hiding it in the bushes. If I didn't know it was there, I'd have missed it which was probably the point.

"When we get inside, let me do the talking," Patrick explained, looping my arm through his as if we were just taking a nightly stroll. "I know it will be hard for you to hold your tongue but please, for both our sakes, try."

The warning look he gave me made me purse my lips. I could keep my mouth shut when I needed to. I wasn't a complete idiot. Plus, I'd just run away. What would I say to them anyway? Oh, yeah, I went to start a revolt, but I'm back now. Yeah. That would work.

"I'm fine with you taking the lead," I told him, holding onto his arm tighter as we got closer to the palace. "But don't think I'll hold my tongue if you say anything that doesn't go with the plan."

Patrick smirked, and I swore he rolled his eyes. "God help me if I go off script." He squeezed the hand on top of his arm and smiled down at me. "Please, for once, just trust me. Everything will be fine."

Pfft. Easy for him to say. His heart wasn't beating like a freight train. Believe me, I could hear it. The reminder that I had super hearing made me take slow deep breaths to try and calm my own rampaging heart. No need to give away the game by accident.

We walked up the path and toward the palace. When we reached the double glass doors, two servants opened them for us with a nod of their head. So far so good. They hadn't even seemed surprised to see me.

"Who knows I was gone?" I muttered, leaning so close to Patrick I could smell the soap on his skin, as well as his own personal scent. I pulled back before I could rub my face against him to inhale it even more profoundly. *Man, get a grip on your hormones, Clara!*

"The Crimson Fold members and Asher obviously," Patrick spoke at a normal volume, not at all worried about being overheard. "We've just told everyone else that you have been sick and cooped up in our room."

"*Our* room?" I squeaked, my eyebrows shooting up my forehead. "When did we get a room?"

"About the time you left," Patrick said, all nonchalantly as if it weren't that big a deal.

I stopped in my tracks, jerking him to a stop with me. "Don't you think that's something you should have told me about before this?" I hissed, trying to keep my voice low so that I didn't attract unwanted attention. "We're not even close to the 'sharing a room' phase."

Patrick clucked his tongue and sighed. "It was the only way to make sure no one checked on you. Now, they think we are helplessly in love, and I am the doting husband, caring for you myself."

My nose wrinkled up and I crossed my arms over my chest. "Well, doesn't that just make you look so great. What about me? How do you think that makes me look?"

Raising a brow, Patrick said, "Like someone who isn't plotting to take down the entire government."

Frowning hard, I tried to think of a good argument but came up empty. With a frustrated huff, I stomped down the hallway, no longer playing the loving couple. I assumed Patrick would follow, not that I bothered to look. It wasn't until I tried to turn toward where Marsha's room was that he stopped me.

"What?" I asked a bit harsher than needed.

Patrick dropped my arm and gestured in the other direction. "Marsha's room is in the other direction."

"No," I said, my lips going into a distinctive oh shape. "His room is this way. I know I've been gone a few days, but really, I think I remember it."

Shaking his head slightly, Patrick said, "Not anymore he doesn't."

"What do you mean, not anymore?"

"I mean—"

"Clarabelle!" a screeching voice I had hoped never to hear again interrupted Patrick.

Teeth clenched together, I turned in slow motion. "Zara. What a surprise to see you."

Zara sauntered over to me, her dark hair slicked back from her face, and the dramatic makeup on her face made her look even more the villain. Thankfully, in this instance, she was fully clothed. I didn't think I could deal with one more spandex outfit. Though she apparently wasn't wearing anything under her suit jacket. When she moved a certain way, I got way more of an eye full than I wanted or ever needed.

"I should be the one surprised." Zara grinned viciously. "Aren't you sick? Oh, wait a second." She put her hand over her mouth with mock surprise. "Don't tell me that wasn't true, and that you've been gone this entire time." The evil glint in her eye told me she didn't really expect an answer, she was just torturing me as per usual.

"Yeah, nice to see you too, Zara." I turned away from her, gesturing to an unamused Patrick to come on.

Unfortunately, Zara wasn't done yet.

"I can't say how sorry I was to hear you'd left. We really thought you two kids would work out." She grinned at Patrick and me, but then did something so completely Zara that I really shouldn't have been surprised. Sliding up against Patrick's side, she dipped her hands beneath his suit jacket, her face a bit too close to his for my comfort. "And our esteemed leader, you are so merciful to put up with our Clarabelle. Please, let me know if there is anything I can do to make up for her behavior. Anything at all." She licked her lips in what I think she meant to be a seductive way but all I could see was my fist through her face.

Before I could make my daydream a reality, Patrick disentangled Zara's hands from him and took a step back. "No, thank you. I am perfectly happy with Clarabelle, my wife." His tone of voice was cold, and even I shivered a bit. To make matters better, he flashed a fang and growled, "And the next time you put your hands on my person or insult Clarabelle in any way, you will find yourself in the dungeon with the rest of the waste of space."

Zara's eyes widened, and I could smell the fear wafting off her. Then as soon as it came, her face hardened, her steely gaze shooting over to me before she turned on her heels and marched away.

My mouth dropped open, and I walked over to Patrick. "I can't believe you did that." I shook my head, a grin spreading across my face. "I mean, I'd always imagined telling her off like that but you just ... you just did it. And it was like ..." I grabbed my head as if to keep my head from exploding. "Boom. You did it." I was so excited I couldn't be held accountable for my actions. I grabbed him by the face and planted one right on his lips.

Patrick grinned at me, bemusement in his eyes. "If I'd known I'd get that kind of reaction, I would have done that sooner."

Smacking him on the shoulder, I rolled my eyes. "Whatever. Let's go before we run into anyone else I might have to stab for touching you."

Following behind Patrick, the closer we got to Marsha's room, the more my mood darkened. We were really going to do this. We were going to try and get Marsha's memories back. What if it didn't work? What if it did? Oh, God. What if he hated me or tried to kill me because of what I'd become? Suddenly, giving him back his memories didn't seem like such a good idea.

"Clarabelle." Patrick placed his hand on my shoulder, turning me to look at him. "It'll be fine. Take deep breaths. If he's really your friend, if he really cares for you the way he claims, he won't hate you."

I glared at him. "Can you stop being so perceptive for a minute and let me freak out?"

Patrick smirked. "Not possible." He stopped us in front of a door and started to knock but stopped, his hand lowering. "This is your last chance. If we go in there, we must do this, and then there is no turning back. We'll be declaring war against the Crimson Fold and all that it entails."

Chewing on my lower lip, I processed what he was saying. Really, I'd already done what he said. So, adding one more sin to the list won't really make a difference. I might as well go out with a bang.

I met Patrick's awaiting gaze and nodded. "I'm sure. Let's do this." Patrick lifted his hand again, but I grabbed it. "Wait, why is his room over here now?"

Frowning, Patrick seemed reluctant to tell me. "Because he shares a room with Tris now. This is her room."

My stomach fell out through my butt, and I was frozen in place. Marsha and Tris shared a room now? As in they were together-together? My eyesight went spotty, and I had to hold onto the door frame so I could catch my breath.

I should have known. What did I expect? Tris, the evil monster, had explicitly erased his memories so she could do this to him.

Did I think she would be content to have him simply hanging off her arm?

"Clarabelle," Patrick murmured soothingly, his hand rubbing circles on my back. "Please, we must hurry. You'll have to have your panic attack later."

Swallowing and nodding at the same time, something that made my head spin, I tried to pull myself together. As Patrick knocked on the door, I looked at him, like really looked at him. How can he stand it? Here Patrick was helping me bring back someone who was his competition, and now he says he loves me. I know there was no way he thought I didn't have feelings for Marsha. He'd have to be dense to do so, and I didn't think Patrick was capable of that. Could someone really be that perfect?

As the door to Marsha's room opened, and the man I'd come to see appeared, I realized something, standing there between the two of them. I might care for Marsha, but I was in love with Patrick. That thought scared me more than anything that was to come.

Chapter 15

MARSHA LOOKED EXACTLY THE way I remembered. Except shirtless. I definitely didn't expect to see him answering the door shirtless.

"Hello," Marsha greeted me blankly and then turned to Patrick, a big smile on his face. "Mr. Blordril, so good to see you. My mistress isn't here right now. Would you like me to call a servant for her?"

I glanced at Patrick with confusion and mouthed 'Mistress?' What the hell had Tris done to him? He hadn't been this bad at the wedding reception. Sure, a bit absent-minded but not like this.

Patrick ignored my silent question and answered Marsha. "No, thank you. We're actually here to see you. You remember

Clarabelle, my wife." He draped an arm over my shoulders.

Recognition came to Marsha's eyes but not the kind I'd hoped for. "Oh, Mrs. Blordril. I'm sorry, I heard you were sick."

"Uh, I was," I fumbled out and then offered a smile. "But as you can see, I'm all better now." I opened my arms as if to say 'tada.'

Marsha nodded politely and then turned his gaze back to Patrick. "So, what did you want to see me about?"

Gesturing inside of the room, Patrick said, "Maybe we should go inside to discuss this. I don't want to disrupt your neighbors."

"Of course, of course." Marsha nodded enthusiastically, moving out of the doorway for us to enter. "Just let me put a shirt on."

While he went and did that, Patrick and I stepped into the room. Tris's room wasn't anything like I expected. Okay, so I hadn't spent a lot of time thinking about what the older vampire woman's bedroom looked like, but if I had to imagine, it wouldn't have been the pink monstrosity before me.

The walls were a muted pink that was offset by the darker shade lining the ceiling and floor. There was a fur rug that could only be described as screaming pink as well as a matching duvet set on the bed. The number of frills decorating the room made me want to gouge my eyes out.

"Tris likes pink, huh?" I couldn't help but say, earning me a warning look from Patrick and a grin from Marsha.

"Oh, yeah. Isn't it great?" Marsha said, buttoning up his shirt over his massive muscles.

I nodded slightly, forcing a smile. "It sure is something."

Either they had erased all sense from his head, or Marsha really was that dense. I was hoping for the prior because I couldn't see him not catching the sarcasm in my voice. Plus, it was just downright evil to make someone like the same color as you to this extent. It just had to be stopped.

Patrick dropped his arm from my shoulders and approached Marsha. "Marsha, how much has your mistress told you about how you came to live here?"

Marsha frowned for a moment and then grinned broadly. "My mistress told me she found me wandering the streets with no memory or clothes. She found me so handsome she couldn't allow me to suffer in such a manner. So, she brought me here and well," - he beamed like a proud father - "here I am!"

Man, Tris really laid it on thick. She couldn't have told him he'd been in an accident, and that's why he didn't remember anything. At least, keep it to the original story, but no, she had to remake him altogether. I was happy I hadn't told his father what had happened to him. He'd have been devastated to see his son like this. I was feeling a bit traumatized myself.

Patrick didn't seem as bothered as I was by Marsha's explanation and just asked, "How would you like to get some of your memories back? It wouldn't take away the memories you have now, just let you remember what happened to you. Why you ended up where you were."

Brows furrowed, Marsha didn't answer at first. "I'm not sure. If my mistress wanted me to have them back, I'd imagine she'd give them to me. She's quite powerful, you know." He said it so matter-of-factly that I didn't think Patrick had the heart to correct him. I knew I wouldn't have.

"I know," Patrick agreed and patted him on the shoulder. "But I have a certain talent for these things and think your mistress would be delighted to know about your life before here. Don't you agree?"

That silly grin was back again, and the urge to knock some sense into Marsha was strong. *Down Clarabelle, down. Let Patrick do his work.*

"That sounds like a great idea." Marsha basically bounced on his heels like a puppy waiting to be petted. "She's always telling me the most fascinating stories, and it would be nice to have something to tell her in return. If you think you can do it, I'd be delighted to have you try."

I grabbed hold of Patrick, dragged him down to my level, and whispered quickly, "Please, please do it quickly before I hit him on principle."

Patrick patted my hand and then withdrew from my grasp, a grim expression on his face. Moving over to Marsha, he said, "Why don't you have a seat? It might make this easier."

"Okay, sure." Marsha did as Patrick asked and sat on a pink flamingo bench. Patrick stood before him and placed his hands on either side of Marsha's head, but before he could do anything, Marsha interrupted, "Will this hurt?"

"It shouldn't," Patrick reassured him. "The main thing to remember is not to fight me. You have to open yourself up to me, or it will be unpleasant for you."

Marsha nodded, and I shifted over toward them so I could watch more clearly.

I'd only heard about vampires being able to get into your mind and had seen the aftermath. I'd never seen it actually performed. It would be a handy skill to have at one point, even if I didn't ever plan to use it.

Patrick seemed to read my mind because his gaze locked onto mine. "As I told Marsha, it is easier if they don't fight you, but it can be done without consent, though it is painful for both parties."

Nodding, I watched intently as Patrick closed his eyes and told Marsha, "Just relax."

I wasn't sure what I was supposed to expect. Some kind of glowing magical power emanating from Patrick's hands? Maybe a few fancy words in another language? Even a humming sound would have been something, but there was not a sound or single indication of what was happening. Just Patrick's slow breathing which was mimicked by Marsha. To me, studying them from the outside, it didn't seem like anything was happening. It wasn't until Marsha's breathing quickened that I knew Patrick was actually doing something.

"No, no." Marsha shook his head, trying to dislodge Patrick's hand. "I've changed my mind. Please, no." The whimper that came from him made me reach my hand out, but Patrick made a noise, causing me to drop it.

Sweat dripped down Patrick's forehead, and his brows furrowed in concentration. Obviously, Marsha's sudden reluctance was making it harder for him. While I didn't like to see either of them in pain, it was good to know that mind raping was a double-edged sword. You couldn't take without getting hurt as well.

Marsha moved his head from side to side, moaning his displeasure. Patrick had a good grip on him, though, and wouldn't let go. Good thing too, because his moaning changed into mumbling and I distinctively think I heard my name in there somewhere.

"It's working," I said, mostly to myself. "I can't believe it's actually working."

No one responded to me though. Not that I expected them to, they were both elbows deep in Marsha's brain. I doubted even if I were bleeding on the ground that they would notice me.

Eventually, the moaning from Marsha stopped, and Patrick seemed not to be in as much pain as before. I hoped that meant they were almost finished. I wasn't sure I could take it anymore. I mean, it wasn't my brain getting put back together, but the waiting was terrible enough that I might as well have been.

Patrick was the one to open his eyes first, then Marsha, who blinked several times before his eyes settled on Patrick. Instead of the kind of giddy grin Patrick had received before now, sharp daggers were shooting from his eyes. Yep, Marsha was back.

Jerking away from Patrick's hands, Marsha shoved the vampire out of the way and moved as far away from us as possible. Marsha paced the floor, his hand on his chin, muttering to himself. It seemed like he was trying to work something out, and I wasn't sure it was my place to interrupt that, no matter how much I wanted to.

His muttering eventually stopped, and he smacked himself on the side of the head before spinning in place and pointing a finger at Patrick, "You! This is all your fault. You did this to me."

"Actually," Patrick corrected, "Tris did this on her own. I simply did not stop her."

"Big difference," Marsha scoffed, his hands balled into fists at his side. He was so angry. I could see it pulsating through his veins and through his body. The rage wafted off of his skin in waves. It made me kind of hungry.

Before I could stop it, my fangs peeked out of my mouth, and Marsha gasped. I quickly covered my mouth and took a step back as he stared at me in horror. Shaking my head, I tried to explain behind my hand. "It's not what you think." Of course, it didn't come out that way. It sounded more like, "It ot awt oh ink." Which made no sense at all.

"Oh, I think it is," Marsha snapped, stomping toward me. Patrick stepped in front of me, blocking me from his view. "I think that while I was being that horrible woman's boy toy, you were off becoming one of the very things we were trying to stop."

I pushed Patrick out of the way. "No, it's not. They took you, Marsha." I tried to show him how distressed it had made me. How helpless I had felt that I couldn't help him. "Then they made me put on a fancy white dress and walk down the aisle, all while I was being watched by everyone we know."

"You didn't have to," Marsha accused. "You could have said no."

"And do what?" I practically yelled. "Let them kill you? Kill my family? Getting married to Patrick was the least of my worries."

Marsha snorted. "Obviously not, because you became like him after all."

"Not by choice!" I screeched, my fingers curling into balls until they bit my skin. The smell of blood tinged in the air and I forced myself to calm down. "Look, I don't want to fight. You should just be happy that we were able to undo what Tris did."

"Oh, yes. Thank you so much for bringing back the misery I'd blissfully forgotten." Marsha crossed his arms over his chest, the sarcasm in his voice drilling into my patience.

"You should be." I turned and gestured at Patrick. "He could have let you rot. He didn't have to fix you. He only did it because I asked him to."

"Because he's using you, don't you see that?" Marsha shook his head in disbelief. "I can't believe that you're just willing to forgive him and forget about everything he has put you through, put me, Violet, and Narq through. And what about Tillie?"

I smiled sadly. "I can't change what's already happened. Patrick has gained my trust, and nothing you will say can change that." I stepped away from him until my back bumped against Patrick's back. His hands came up to rest on my shoulders. "Besides, it's too late for any of that. Alban knows. They'll be attacking any time now. I only wanted to make sure you were fixed before it all went down."

"Well, I am." Marsha made a disgusted noise and looked down, shaking his head. "You can have peace of mind knowing you 'fixed' me."

"Marsha ..." I started, but he put up his hand cutting me off.

"No, don't. I can't even look at you without thinking about what you are now." His eyes were so full of emotion that it hurt. "The things she did to me. I can still remember them. I liked it, Clara. They didn't just make me forget, they took me over. How you can be with one of them, after everything? I can't forgive that. It'd have been better if you had never given me my memory back at all."

I opened my mouth to tell him that he didn't mean that, but Patrick's hand on my shoulder tightened. He was right. I'd done what I had set out to do. The end result wasn't something I had wanted, but I guess I couldn't expect to get everything I wanted. The only thing I could do now was hope for the best and let Marsha go. After all, he'd already done the same.

Chapter 16

WE WERE BOTH QUIET as Patrick walked me back to the tunnel. I think he knew I had a lot on my mind, another sign of his being able to read me so well. I wondered if he had always been that way, or if it was because of his blood? I'd like to think I'd been harder to read when I was human.

"Are you going to go back to your father's now?" Patrick touched my arm, stopping me from entering the tunnel.

I glanced down at his hand and then slowly to his face. I honestly wasn't sure what I'd do. I didn't want to go back, just to lay there awake thinking about what Marsha said. Just thinking about doing that was too depressing. I also didn't want to stay here. My father and the other leaders looked ready to storm the castle at any moment. I didn't think this was a very safe place for me to be.

"I might go to my stepmother's," I said finally. "I haven't seen them since the wedding, and I doubt they know what's going on." I paused for a moment, a sad smile on my lips. "We might not have ever gotten along well, but I can't let them get caught in the crossfire. I've caused enough people pain as it is."

"Clarabelle." The way Patrick said my name made tears well up, and I put my hand up to stop him from coming closer. If he touched me, I just knew I'd fall apart.

"Please don't," I muttered, turning away from him. "I just can't. Not right now."

"You know it's not your fault," Patrick said anyway, his hand on my shoulder. "Marsha is angry now, but he will not be forever. Maybe you will be able to find peace between you."

I nodded numbly. I was pretty sure Patrick was wrong. The anger in Marsha's eyes hadn't just been because I had forgiven Patrick, but because of what I'd become. We'd never be the same way we had been before. My vampirism would always block the way of any kind of friendship we could have had, forget anything else.

No, I had to resign myself to the fact that Marsha was safe and that's all I could hope for. I had a new life now. I wouldn't get to keep everyone safe and have them too. After all, I was a vampire. I had forever, and they had maybe fifty, sixty years at most? What kind of friendship would that be? How I ever thought we could have anything now that I was one of them baffled me. And pissed me off.

"Clarabelle," Patrick tried once more, but I'd had enough.

"No, Patrick. Just stop." I shook his hand away. "Marsha was right. I'm a monster now. I can't expect anyone to see me as anything other than that."

Patrick sighed dejectedly. "But I do not see you that way. Nor do I believe your father does."

"Doesn't count." I shook my head bitterness in my voice. "None of it will matter after this is all said and done. We'll be lucky not to be dead in any case." With that, I opened the tunnel door and marched inside, slamming it shut behind me.

Patrick thankfully didn't follow me. I couldn't handle any more of his understanding. I just needed to wallow for a while. I was in an impossible situation of my own creation. Sure, I'd had good intentions, but you know what they say about those.

I'd ended up becoming the thing I wanted to save the rest of Alban from, only to turn around and betray them as well. Does what people see me as decide who I should be loyal to? Should I be for the humans or the monsters? To Marsha or to Patrick? The questions were really all one and the same.

Of course, I knew I was being pessimistic, but I really didn't see how this was going to turn out good for me. Either I would end up getting killed in the midst of Alban's revolution, or I'd have to hide away. I didn't see the common people letting only a few of us vampires live. I wouldn't if I was them. I'd have said to kill them all and let the pieces fall where they may.

Part of me wondered what exactly my father and the others planned to do after they took back Alban. Did they have a plan? Would they change the way we divided the food and resources? Would they elect a new leader? Or would everything fall apart and end up even worse than it had been before?

My mind whirled with so many thoughts that I almost missed the exit for the Inner Circle. I pushed the tunnel door open and walked through the town, my arms wrapped around myself as if they could protect me from my dark thoughts. It hadn't been that long since I'd left the Glade, there should have still been people on the streets. When I'd lived here before, there would be people partying until the early morning hours. The fact that it was so quiet didn't sit well with me.

Turning away from the quiet marketplace, I started toward my stepmother's new house. I didn't know exactly where it was but figured there couldn't be too many new houses in the upper part of town. Maybe they put a sign up like they did at their old house. I could only be so lucky.

The upper part of town wasn't much different from the rest of the Inner Circle, except that the houses were bigger and there weren't any shops. They left that to the riff-raff of downtown. I rolled my eyes. Even the elite had their lessers. When would everyone realize that we were all the same? We all bled the same blood. What we had didn't make us any different or better than anyone else.

I walked down the street, peeking in windows like a creep until I found my little sister, Lea, perched in a window. She had a book in her hand and a girly smile on her lips. She must be in a good mood. At least, one of us was.

She must have sensed me watching her because she looked up from her book and saw me. Her eyes widened, and a broad grin spread across her face. Lea jumped from her seat and came bounding out the door.

"Clara!" she screeched so loudly, I swore the sleeping neighbors heard her. She wrapped her arms around my torso and pressed her head to my chest in a tight hug. Placing my hand on her back. I patted her, not really in the hugging mood.

"Hey, Lea." I forced a smile onto my lips. "How are you?"

She pulled back from me and giggled. "I'm fantastic. You can't believe all the amazing things that have happened to me since you left. It's like a dream come true. You know Derek Bloomberg? The florist's son?" I nodded though I had no idea who she was talking about. "He wants me to go to a dance with him. A real dance with big dresses and everything. I'm so excited."

Her happiness washed over me, and I couldn't help but be happy for her. "I'm glad. You should go to a dance or two before you get married."

"So, what's it like?" she asked, grabbing my hand and dragging me inside. "To be married to Patrick Blordril?"

I shrugged as I stopped in the foyer of the house. There was a grand staircase and a tall ceiling where a crystal fixture hung from the ceiling sparkled in the light.

"It's a lot bigger than our other house huh?" Lea smiled, seeing me look around.

I nodded. "Yeah, it is."

"Lea, who's at the door?" my stepmother walked into the foyer. When she saw me, she came to a halt, her eyes narrowing suspiciously. "Clarabelle, what a surprise. We weren't expecting to see you so soon."

"I know," I said, not letting her intimidate me. "It wasn't planned. I just thought I'd stop by."

"Well, isn't that nice. How long do you plan on staying?" The tight smile on my stepmother's lips told me all I needed to know about what she thought of my visit. I was an unwelcome nuisance she wanted gone as soon as possible.

"Not long," I assured her. "I actually wanted to talk to you all about something important."

"Oh really?" Belinda arched a perfectly shaped brow. "Should I get Julianna?"

"Yes." I inclined my head. "That would be a good idea since it involves all of you."

Lips pressed into a thin line, my stepmother left the room and then shortly after returned with my other stepsister. When Julianna saw me, she didn't seem as upset to see me as I'd have expected. She actually looked relieved.

"Clara," she breathed and pulled me into a surprising hug. "I'm so happy to see you."

"Uh, likewise," I said awkwardly.

Julianna let me go with a knowing look that I didn't understand before going to stand by her mother.

"Very well, we're all here." My stepmother gave Julianna a curious look before staring at me. "Say what you need to. We were just about to call it a night."

"No, we weren't," Lea argued, earning her a warning look from her mother.

Ignoring the poorly veiled hint to leave, I said, "Why don't we sit down? This isn't something to be discussed standing in the doorway."

My stepmother seemed like she might argue but instead straightened her shoulders and nodded curtly. "Fine. This way."

My stepsisters and I followed her into the sitting room where they had a new couch and chairs. It seemed like the house wasn't the only thing they had upgraded.

"As you can see, we have done very well for ourselves because of your marriage." My stepmother couldn't help but point that out. Her words on my wedding day still rang true in my mind, and it took everything in me not to turn around and walk out that door, leaving them to fend for themselves.

"I see that." I nodded politely. Who said I couldn't be mature?

"So, Clara." Julianna crossed one leg over the other, the pretty dress she wore spreading out around her. "What did you want to tell us?"

"Are you pregnant?" Lea shouted out without warning.

"Lea!" her mother and sister chastised her.

I smiled and chuckled. "No, I'm not pregnant." Though, at this point that would have been a happy alternative. The thought of little babies with Patrick made my face heat. I pushed those thoughts away and focused on the challenging task before me.

Taking a deep breath, I started, "Things are happening. They're already in motion, and you can't stop it." I looked at my stepmother to make sure she knew I was talking to her. "The condensed version is the Crimson Fold isn't who you think they are, and the other sections are coming together to stop them."

"What in God's name are you talking about?" my stepmother cried out, outrage on her face. "How dare you come in here talking of some war that you no doubt are the start of!"

I couldn't argue with her there.

Then a startling statement came from Julianna. "I know."

Belinda, Lea, and I all turned as one to look at the oldest daughter. My brows scrunched together, I asked, "What do you mean, you know?"

Julianna shifted uncomfortably in her seat, her eyes dipping down before coming back up, a fierce determination in them. "I mean, I overheard your father talking to some of the others around here. I asked him about it, and he told me the truth. About the election. About the Crimson Fold. About everything." Her eyes settled on me so firmly, and I knew without a doubt he had told her what I was now.

"Why would he tell you and not me?" Belinda gasped. She seemed more upset about the fact that my father had left her out of the loop, rather than the chaos that was about to rain down on us. It was typical for her, really.

Ignoring my stepmother's outrage, I turned to Julianna. "You know that you might not be safe here anymore? When it starts, they might try and come after you."

Julianna nodded. "I know. Richard and I have already discussed options. We have a few places we know we can hide out until the majority of the fighting dies down. Once they're all gone, it'll be easier to talk reason and find a new way to govern that's fair to all."

I was surprised with my stepsister. I never expected her to have two brain cells to rub together that didn't have something to do with dresses or the latest gossip. The fact that she seemed to know exactly what she was doing put me more at ease than anything anyone had said to me. I knew that if I couldn't, Julianna would be able to keep them safe.

Chapter 17

JULIANNA HELPED ME TO the door despite my stepmother's insistence of throwing me out on my ungrateful backside. Lea was left asking a million questions, something for which her mother gave me a good glare.

"So ..." Julianna let out a little laugh. "I guess I've been demoted to your level now."

I quirked a brow and smirked. "It's not so bad down here."

"Tell that to my mother." Julianna rolled her eyes, crossing her arms over her chest. "You'd think I'd done something atrocious like becoming a vampire or something."

We exchanged a look and then burst out laughing. I'd never expected to finally connect with my stepsister. Especially not like this but I was happy I did. It made things a little bit easier, knowing she was on my side. Even if I never got to see her or the rest of them ever again.

"Yeah, that would be horrible. Just unheard of." I wiped the tears of laughter from my eyes. After a moment, when we stopped laughing, I sighed. "So, are you really going to be okay?"

Julianna glanced back to the house and then back to me. "Yeah, I think we will. I mean, I can't see the future or anything, and I know there will be some trying times ahead, but I think we'll be fine. What about you?" She inclined her head to me. "What are you going to do?"

I shrugged. "I don't know yet. I'll figure it out, I guess. Kind of depends on how this whole thing goes down." The first sign will be them coming at me with an ax, then I'll know if I should run or not. My biggest worry was that I wouldn't be able to figure it out until it was too late.

"What about Patrick?" Julianna bumped my shoulder. "He's one too, right?"

"Yeah. He changed me," I said lowly. "And I used to hate him for it, but now, I know he's just like me, put in an impossible situation with no easy choice."

"Does it feel any different?" She cocked her head to the side. "You know, being a vampire."

I smiled slightly. "A bit. There's the blood thing, of course, but other than heightened senses, I feel normal." I chuckled darkly. "Well, as normal as I've ever felt."

"Well, there's something to be said for that and hey," - she placed her hand on my arm and grinned cheekily - "at least, you'll never have to worry about wrinkles."

Snorting, I dragged Julianna into a tight hug. "I wish we'd had the time to get to know each other."

"Me too," she murmured in my ear. "Who knows? We might still get that chance."

I pulled back and gave her a tight smile. "I'm sure we will."

I could tell by the sad look she gave me that she didn't really believe it, but I had to say it anyway. We lied to each other like we lied to ourselves, because otherwise, what did we have to live for?

"I better get going." I released her and started back down the path. "I'll see you around?"

Julianna lifted a hand. "Yeah, I'll see you."

Nodding in response, I turned away from her and forced myself not to look back. It didn't matter what we said or what we wanted to happen, the next few days would unfold with or without our blessing. I just prayed we'd all be alive to see the end of it.

The walk back to the tunnel was a depressing one. Seeing my stepfamily had really put things in perspective for me. No matter the outcome of this fight, I didn't think I'd be able to see them again. At least not for a while. The most significant problem was where to go until then?

As I approached the trees hiding the entrance to the tunnel, I heard a noise. A rush of hushed whispers and clanking metal. I darted behind a tree and focused on what they were saying.

"Are you sure they are ready?" a voice I recognized as Nex asked. "I mean, Richard told us to wait until morning."

"Stop your worrying," another voice, Quell's, snapped. "This is our fight. You heard what he said. He can't be trusted to be unbiased."

"But it's his daughter," Nex argued, and then grunted as if he'd been hit.

"That's exactly why he doesn't need to be leading this attack," Dale growled out with what sounded like a stamp of his foot. "He'll be worried about getting her to safety, not taking down the monsters."

"They all need to die." The pure hatred in Quell's voice made me shudder. He really hated us, and he hadn't even met the worst of the vampires. A petty part of me hoped he'd find out just how horrible we could be before the night was over.

"Look we don't have time for this," Dale reminded them. "The others will be here any minute now. Then we're going to rush them."

I started to wonder how many people they really had when a flurry of voices filled the air. I couldn't pick the voices apart but knew there were enough in there that they could do some real damage.

I hid in my hiding spot until they finished gathering, my heart pounding in my chest. My feet itched to get going, but I couldn't risk them catching me. They might not have enough to take the whole Crimson Fold down, but they definitely had enough to take me down.

"Finally, let's go," Quell snarled, and their feet pounded down into the tunnel, their voices beginning to fade into the darkness below. I moved slowly from my spot toward the entrance, but before I could get out of the trees, a hand clamped over my mouth. My eyes widened, and I whipped around, my hand flying through the air. I managed to pull my punch back even as the distinctive head of my father ducked before my fist hit him in the face.

"What are you doing here?" I whispered quietly, my eyes searching around us. "Why aren't you back in the Glade?"

My father frowned, a severe look on his face. "You mean, why aren't I left behind by those idiots who think they are so smart?" He shook his head with a fierceness in his eyes. "Mara overheard them and came and told me about their plans to attack tonight. And I couldn't ..." He grabbed my hands tightly, his eyes full of emotion. "I couldn't let them get you. I had to warn you. So, I snuck away before they were planning on leaving and have been searching for you ever since."

"How'd you find me?" I wrapped my arms around his waist and hugged him tightly.

"Julianna." He held me close. "I went to the house, and she mentioned you'd just left. Alas, here I am."

"Well, I have to say I'm happy to see you, especially after that mob came through." I pointed toward the tunnel door still left ajar. "I barely missed them. I could have been their first victim." The very thought made me more depressed than what had happened with Marsha.

"What are you going to do?"

"Don't worry about me. What about you?" I asked, glancing up at him with

184

sadness in my voice. "I mean, they think you'll be too lenient. They might come after you after all this."

"I'm going to get your stepmother and stepsisters and get them to safety first." He explained, brushing my hair away from my face. "Then I am going to find Mara, and we're going to gather the sane leaders from the other sections and figure out what we are going to do when this is all over."

"You're not going to join the fight?" I asked, cocking my head to the side. "I'd have thought you'd want to get a piece of the action."

My father shook his head. "No, I'm too old for that. Violence only causes more violence. I'll let the other hotheads take care of it. I'm going to focus on keeping everyone safe."

"What about the ones in the dungeon?" I reminded him. "There's a whole room of people who won't know what's going on. Heck, that mob might not even realize what's wrong with them and might go slashing heads without asking." I chopped my hand through the air to illustrate my point.

"I suppose I could gather a group to search for them." My father stroked his chin as he thought about it. "That way, someone is there when the crazies start showing up, but how are we going to fix those people?" he asked, his eyes boring into me. "Were you able to fix Marsha?"

I coughed at the mention of Marsha and cleared my throat a couple of times. "Yeah, yes. We did. As far as fixing them, I think it will have to wait until the dust settles, you know?" I licked my lips and tried to figure out how to explain. "I've never done what Patrick did, so I wouldn't know the first thing about fixing them or even if they can all be fixed. With the angry mob out there, I'm not so sure we'll be welcome near here for a while, even to give them their minds back."

"I understand." My father nodded. A shout in the distance drew his attention. "You should probably get going. They have probably made it to the Core by now. If you leave now, you'll be able to get out before they even finish going through the palace."

Swallowing thickly, I pushed back the tears. He didn't need to see me cry. I needed to be strong for him. He had enough to worry about, he didn't need me in the mix.

"Clarabelle," he said, stopping me from leaving. "Just promise me, when you get somewhere safe and when this is all over, you'll let me know you're okay?"

I smiled at him and nodded. "I promise."

"Good. Now, get out of here." He gave me a little push away from the tunnel. "Don't go that way. There will still be some in there looking for your kind trying to escape."

"Gotcha." I held his hand tightly and then, with a deep breath, let it go. It seemed I had to do a lot of that lately. It was something I was going to have to get used to and quickly.

I darted into the darkness, not stopping until I couldn't see my father any longer. I reached the wall between the Inner Circle and the Core. What was I doing? I hadn't told my father because I didn't know. I'd planned to get away but had no idea where. I knew I couldn't leave Patrick behind. Also, Asher was still in there. If I had a chance to save them from the coming attack I needed to do it now.

Glancing around behind me, I made sure no one was looking before I bent my knees and jumped. I scaled the wall the same way I did the first time after I turned. This time my speed and agility didn't surprise me enough to make me stop at the top. Instead, I dropped over the other side and landed in a crouch off to the side of the palace. From where I was standing, I couldn't be too far from the Core tunnel entrance, meaning I had to move fast.

As I crept through the hedges and trees, I heard yelling and pounding of feet. There were shots from blaster guns in the distance. I wasn't sure if they were from our side or theirs. If they had been smart, they would have convinced the guards to turn on the Fold first, but I wasn't so sure they did that.

I waited behind a large bush for an opening to get to the palace. Half a dozen men and women attacked one of the servants. I was pretty sure they weren't a vampire, but they didn't seem to care. They beat them to the ground and then chopped their head off.

When the blood tinged the air, my fangs ached. I forced my thirst back. This was not the time to get all fang happy. This was the time to play human. Human would keep me alive.

After they made sure the servant was dead, the mob ran around the side of the castle. That was my chance, and I took it. I bolted from my hiding spot and into the side door of the castle.

The inside was worse than outside. Blood soaked the air and the ground. Bodies of servants and companions alike were left discarded in the hallway. Some of them without heads, others with their hearts pierced through with blaster bolts. Apparently, they had indeed gotten some guards on their sides.

Not allowing myself to waste time on mourning for the mistaken humans, I rushed to Asher's room. He was closest. Besides, Patrick knew the revolutionaries were coming. He had to have a plan, right? Right?

Chapter 18

I WALKED DOWN THE halls with a purpose. I didn't use my super speed, at least not out in the open like this. It would just draw attention to myself.

The carnage was far more than I ever expected. Not that I really knew what to expect, to be fair. I'd never been in a fight. I didn't know what war looked like, but the further into the palace I got, the more bodies there were on both sides.

A gurgling noise stopped me as I made my way down the hall. Moving toward the sound, I realized it was coming from a person. As I came closer, I realized that it wasn't just anyone, it was Dale. His eyes looked around him wildly, and his mouth gaped open and shut. When he saw me, he didn't move, just kept moving his mouth as if he were trying to say something to me. Looking down from his head, I grimaced.

It looked like someone had reached into his neck and ripped his throat out. This could only be the work of a vampire. It seemed like Dale had mouthed off to the wrong person, and they had done precisely what I'd imagined doing myself a time or two.

Despite our differences, I sat by him until the gurgling stopped and his mouth stayed open. He was gone. Reaching out, I brushed my hand over his eyes closing them. A horrible way to go.

Standing to my feet, I glanced around. It seemed this area had been worked over already. There wasn't anyone around to worry about having my head cut off, or my heart ripped out. Unfortunately, that meant they were working faster than I gave them credit for. I expected the vampires to put up more of a fight. Of course, so far, I'd only see the human victims.

Rounding a corner, I had only a split second to duck before an ax came swinging at my head. With my cover blown, I was suddenly surrounded by three angry mob members from the corridor ahead. They jeered at me, poking out at me with their makeshift weapons. One had a pitchfork, while another had a hoe. The one with the ax twisted it in his hand, a nasty grin on his lips.

"Come on, now." I held my hands up and backed away from them. "I'm one of you."

"No, you're not." The one with the ax growled. "You're married to that Blordril, meaning you're one of them."

"Hey, you can't blame that on me." I pointed a finger at him, trying to make him see reason. "I was forced to do that. I didn't have much choice in the matter."

"Still, vampire or not, anyone associated with the Fold has to die."

This was the nonsense Quell was putting in people's heads? No wonder there were so many casualties. They weren't just going for vampires, they were going for anyone they saw. There was no reasoning with that level of crazy.

I wasn't a fighter. I'd never gotten into a fight in my life, not counting the little scuffle with Zara at the ball. That'd been more of a hair-pulling incident, not a 'pointy end in the soft flesh' battle. I did know that I was faster than them, stronger than them, and that had to give me some sort of advantage.

"Enough talking," The one with the pitchfork snapped and, with a yell, charged at me.

I jumped to the side and grabbed the pitchfork by the handle, swinging the man around with it until he slammed into the wall. I didn't have time to see if he was out because the others decided to come at me at the same time. An ax swung at my head, and the hoe went for my body. I dropped to the ground and kicked my leg out, knocking the ax guy onto his back.

The one with the hoe seemed enraged by my actions and started swinging at me wildly. I grabbed the end of the hoe, the sharp end of it cutting into my hand. We played tug of war for a moment before I jerked it hard, taking it from his hands. Now that I was armed, the others weren't so confident in themselves. Flashing my fangs, I dared them to come after me again.

Instead, they jumped to their feet and ran in the opposite direction, all except the one I had slammed into the wall. My nose prickled, and I slowly turned to see blood seeping from the man's head. Having just been injured, my fangs ached for me to feed.

I dropped the hoe and started toward him, unable to resist the call of the blood. I knelt beside him and drew back to bite him, my stomach rumbling its encouragement. Before I could strike, I was jerked away from the body. With a snarl, I twisted my head around to snap at whoever stopped me.

"It's me. Clarabelle, it's me." Marsha held his hands up, fear in his eyes.

I forced myself to relax and put my fangs away. Standing up with Marsha, I searched for him for any sign of injury. Seeing he was as he should be, I asked, "What are you doing here? You should have run by now."

Marsha snorted. "I could say the same about you."

"I had to get Asher and Patrick," I told him, not letting his disgusted look make me feel bad. "They're my friends. I'm not just going to leave them."

"And what about me? Or Violet?" Marsha snapped, his hands curling into fists. "Were you going to just leave us?"

I shook my head. "I didn't know they were just taking everyone out. I thought they'd go for the vampires and that's it."

"Well, they are," Marsha bit out, anger coloring his face. "I was able to gather a few of the companions and helped them out into the Inner Circle. Thankfully, some of the idiots out there aren't too consumed by the bloodlust to see reason."

"That's good." I nodded, and then when shouts sounded like they were coming toward us, I said, "Come on, we can't stay here."

With a nod of agreement, Marsha followed me down the hallway. We were almost to Asher's room, and by the body count, a sinking feeling filled my stomach. *Please God, don't let us be too late.*

We didn't come across any resistance as we came up to Asher's room. Marsha started to open the door, but I stopped him. Looking up at me curiously, I said, "He might think it's an attack, better knock first."

Nodding, Marsha stepped aside. I knocked on the door and called out, "Asher, are you in there? It's me. Clarabelle."

There was some movement inside and then silence. I frowned, my brows furrowed in confusion. Exchanging a look with Marsha, I reached out to open the door, but suddenly, the door was thrown open.

Asher stood in the doorway, the lower half of his face covered in blood. He glanced at Marsha and me before ushering us in quickly. His head peeked out to check the hallway, and then he shut the door firmly behind him.

"Clara," Asher gasped, pulling me into his arms. "You can't believe how happy I am to see you."

Letting him hug me, I grinned. "I can imagine." Pulling away from him, I asked, "Where are the girls?"

Asher glanced toward Marsha for a moment, suspicion on his face. "You have your memories back, don't you?"

"Is it that obvious?" Marsha scratched the back of his head, the boy I knew from the marketplace coming out of his hard exterior.

"Patrick did it earlier," I told Asher and then shook him slightly. "Asher, where are your girls?"

Again, he avoided the question. "We should really get away from here. They've passed through once, but they might come back again." He tried to head for the door, but I stopped him, my hand holding fast to his wrist. He looked down at my hand and then back to my face. As if a dam had broken, so did Asher. He fell to his knees and tears poured down his face.

"Asher, Asher," I cooed, kneeling with him. "It's okay. Tell me what happened."

"I couldn't protect them," Asher told me through his sobbing. "They came in while we were sleeping. I'd gone to speak to Patrick and didn't even know we were under attack until I felt them." He gripped his chest tightly. "After you've been together as long as we have, we have sort of a connection, you know?" I nodded, though I didn't really know what he was talking about. "I could feel their pain. Their screaming. I raced back here, but I was too late. They were already dead."

"And the blood?" Marsha gestured toward the front of Asher's shirt and face. "Whose is that?"

A wicked grin curled up Asher's face. "I might not have gotten here in time to save them, but I did catch their killers." Licking his lips, he purred. "They were delicious."

I could tell Asher's words freaked Marsha out, so I said, "Why don't you go get cleaned up? It'll be easier to get you out if you don't look so much like a—"

"Rampaging monster," Marsha filled in, and I glared at him.

"Very well," Asher stood and headed to the bathroom, not really bothered by Marsha's comment.

"Will you hold in your judgment just a little bit?" I demanded, climbing to my feet.

"But he is a rampaging monster," Marsha countered, his arms crossed over his chest.

"What he is, is someone who just lost everyone he cared about in one night. Of course, he'd be a little bit upset." I growled and stepped closer to him. "Have a little compassion."

"I can't." Marsha shook his head. "Not for them." His eyes locked on mine. "Not even for you."

I sighed and took a step back. "Then maybe you should just go. If it comes down to them or us, I can't trust you will choose the right people to save."

Marsha opened his mouth to argue, but clamped it shut and gave me a curt nod. I didn't watch him as he started for the door. It wasn't until he said my name that I turned around.

"You would have loved me, you know. We'd have been happy."

I offered Marsha a small smile, too tired to really get into it. "I know."

Lips pressed together, Marsha nodded again and then he was gone.

I didn't have the energy to cry for what we could have had. There wasn't any time in any case. All I could do was keep moving forward.

"Where'd Marsha go?" Asher asked when he emerged from the bathroom, freshly cleaned of blood. He'd even changed his shirt.

"He's gone." I left it at that and Asher didn't ask. "Let's go. Marsha got a lot of the companions out already. I want to find Patrick."

Following after me, Asher said, "He was in his office last time I saw him. The fighting hadn't gotten up there yet."

I peeked out into the hallway and searched for any attackers. When the coast was clear, I glanced at Asher over my shoulder, "Let's hope that it stayed that way."

Chapter 19

MY WISH THAT THE fighting hadn't gotten that far was dashed as we rushed up the body-littered stairs. We got into a couple of squabbles, but nothing serious enough to stop us.

When we got to the hall Patrick's office was on, I was happy to see the body of Victor lying on the ground, his heart ripped out. With a smug look, I kicked his body out of the way. Even if I hadn't been the one to kill him, I was happy someone had.

"Come on!" Asher grabbed my arm. "You can't gloat without a head."

Rolling my eyes, but quickening my pace, I let Asher pull me down the hallway. Before we could reach Patrick's office, a high-pitched scream stopped us in our tracks. The sound came from an open bedroom door near us. I moved toward it, against my better judgment.

Inside, Beaford laid in two pieces in the middle of the floor. Zara was cornered by a group of three men, her face bloodied and her clothes torn. When I stepped into the room, her eyes shot up to me.

"Clarabelle! Help me." She reached a hand out toward me. The men surrounding her turned as one to look in my direction. One of them was Nex, trembling with nerves from the moment he saw me.

"Just turn around and leave," he urged me. "I have no quarrel with you. Your father is a good man, I'm sure he'd be happy to see you leave this place alive."

A part of me wanted to leave her there, believe that it would be some form of justice to let her die at the hands of the humans, the way she had caused so many other deaths just to get where she was now. No one would blame me or even care if I let her die.

But you would.

Sighing at my own bleeding heart, I took a step closer. "Sorry, Nex. I can't do that."

Zara visibly sagged at my words, but the men around her tensed. Nex didn't seem to want to fight me, but he wasn't backing down either. I felt Asher coming in behind me, causing the men to start to tremble. One vampire was one thing, but two? I think they were about to crack, either to fight or to flee.

"Clarabelle," Asher said at my side, glancing over the scene. "Do you need some help?"

I smirked, letting my fangs slip out, flashing the room. "Sure, I'd be happy for some."

With a battle cry, one of the men came barreling toward us, his weapon held high. As if his shout had been the reassurance the other needed, that one charged as well. Only Nex stayed behind. The coward.

I didn't even get a chance to take the guys out. Asher stepped in front of me, grabbed the guy by the head, and twisted. A sickening crack filled the room and he went limp. Asher dropped him to the ground.

The other one was a bit smarter and tried to shoot Asher with his blaster gun. Too bad he was a crap marksman. The blistering shot went wide, and before the shooter could get another shot off, Asher took hold of the barrel of the gun and jerked it back to hit the man in the face. Blood sprayed from his nose, making him let go of the gun and clutch his face. Asher used the weapon like a club to beat him over the back of the head, knocking him out cold. Or dead, I couldn't really tell.

All that was left was Nex.

"Hey, now." Nex dropped his weapon and held his hands up as we moved in on him. "I'm just following orders."

I scoffed. "You mean the orders to kill innocent bystanders who knew nothing of what was going on? Or maybe the orders to disobey my father and take matters into your own crazy hands?" I reached out, my fingers wrapping around his neck. "Which order are we talking about?"

"All of them." He gasped as I squeezed slightly. "Please, please. Have mercy."

I glanced at Zara who had frozen against the wall, watching me with a mixture of fear and admiration. "Were you going to have mercy on her?" I turned him slightly so he could see Zara's bloodied face. Then without a word, I put my other hand on the back of his head and twisted until there was a crack. Nex sagged in my hands, and I let go of him, making him fall to the ground.

Zara moved slowly away from the wall, her mouth agape. "I can't believe you saved me."

"Don't mention it." I turned on my heel and started for the door. A hand grabbed my elbow, and I twisted around to see Zara standing there.

"Really, Clarabelle. I'm sorry. I can't thank you enough." The genuine gratitude in her eye should have been enough, but it didn't bring those people she killed back. It didn't make up for trying to kill me on more than one occasion. All it did was make me angry.

"Seriously." I jerked my arm away. "Don't mention it."

I stalked out the door and toward Patrick's office. I didn't know if Asher was following me, and at that point, I didn't care. I just wanted to find Patrick and leave. I wanted it all to be over.

The door to Patrick's office wasn't open. I didn't knock this time. Patrick would feel me coming. I expected to see a fight in progress or even Patrick already dead. What I didn't expect was to see Quell bound and gagged in a chair while Patrick sat at his desk as calm as can be.

When I entered, Patrick looked up from his desk. "Ah, Clarabelle. There you are. I hope you didn't run into too much trouble."

The humorous glint in his eye made me laugh. A full-throated 'oh my God, I'm too tired for this crap' laugh. Wiping my face with the back of my hand, I shook my head. "No, not too much trouble."

Asher came running into the room next. He took one look at the scene and frowned. "Why haven't you killed this one?" He pointed at Quell who struggled against his binds, his eyes full of hatred.

Patrick stood and walked around his desk. Leaning against the edge of it, he pointed his clasped hands at Quell. "I am trying to show this one that not all of us are monsters. That the few that have strayed from the path do not define the many, but as you can see," - he smiled darkly - "I am having a difficult time convincing him."

I looked to Quell and then back to Patrick. "This is pointless. I understand what you are trying to do, but this isn't really the time." I moved over to Patrick and took his hands in mine. "We need to leave. Let them figure it out, and when everything calms down, we can try and convince them of our good intentions. After all, someone has to fix the mind-blasted people in the dungeon."

Patrick arched a brow and then nodded. "Very well. Let us leave this place."

I let out a breath, relieved that he didn't argue. To my surprise, he didn't head toward the door but his bookcase. He pulled a book down that caused a click and then a whirling sound. The bookshelf shifted on its own to reveal a door.

Gaping at it, I asked, "Where does that go?"

Patrick chuckled. "You don't think I didn't have a backup plan?"

He ushered Asher and me forward. We followed him inside where he clicked a button which closed the bookshelf behind us. The last thing I saw was Quell's furious face staring at us before the secret door closed on him.

"Where does this go?" Asher's voice bounced off the walls, echoing back at us. The path began to descend, and I could barely hear the fighting still going on in the palace.

"Out of Alban," Patrick explained, "and into the forest around it."

"What do you plan for us to do there?" Asher speculated. There was a dim light in the hidden passage, so it was easy to see the lifting of his brow and the tension in his body. I didn't blame him. We were going out to the unknown. The wild areas surrounding Alban. Who knew what kind of dangers awaited us there?

Patrick lifted an elegant shoulder. "To be honest, I do not know. We can't stay here, as you well know. There's a safe house a few miles away from Alban's border where we can stay until we decide on a more definite plan."

"But for how long?" Asher sighed, dragging a hand through his hair. "We can't stay there forever. And what would we eat?"

"Animals," I told him, earning me a curious look. "We can survive on animals until we can come back. It's not ideal, but it can be done."

Patrick nodded, pride in his face at my suggestion. "As Clarabelle has said, there are other options than taking human life, which we will now have to learn for ourselves."

Asher grew quiet, his questions answered for now. I hoped his mind was more peaceful than mine, which kept whirling at all that was going on.

We were past the bottom floor of the palace and were now at the dungeon level. My father would be in there, taking care of the those who couldn't take care of themselves. I sent a silent prayer to whoever was listening that he was able to get out okay. I wanted to be the hero and save everyone, but sometimes you had to just settle for saving yourself.

Chapter 20

THE SAFE HOUSE HAD been exactly where Patrick had told us. When we reached it, we were beyond exhausted. I only took a moment to check out my home for the foreseeable future.

It was two stories with a beat-up exterior, but it was a high-tech wonderland inside. There were several bedrooms, a kitchen, and even an area set up to be a fully-stocked infirmary. Electricity buzzed through the whole building. Where that power came from was a question that sprang to mind, but I was too tired to ask. I'd leave that and so many more questions for later.

When I woke, it was dark again. I'd slept the rest of the night and through the next day. I went to the bathroom attached to the room I had crashed in and cleaned off my face. I didn't bother to shower right away, not with my stomach growling urgently.

Making my way down the stairs, I heard Patrick and Asher talking quietly with someone else. As I rounded the corner I saw Maleria sitting with them at the kitchen table. I cleared my voice to announce my arrival, though I was sure Patrick already sensed it.

Patrick's head turned to me, and he stood. "Clarabelle, I hope you slept well."

I nodded and then shrugged. "As well as can be expected." I glanced at Maleria. "Is Violet ...?"

Maleria brushed her long blonde hair over her shoulder and smiled softly. "She's fine. Your friend, Marsha, helped get her out."

"Why didn't you bring her with you?" I asked, taking a seat between Patrick and Asher. Patrick handed me a cup, and the distinctive smell of blood wafted up from it. Glancing down at it, I took a tentative sip. "This isn't animal blood." It was more of a statement than a question.

"No," Patrick shook his head with a small smile. "We had a few reserves here for emergencies. It won't last us long, but it will be enough to help us through the transition to animal blood."

Asher made a disgusted noise. "Who thought we'd be reduced to this? Feeding on animals?"

"What else would you have us do?" Patrick asked, a hard edge to his voice. Apparently, they'd had this discussion before. "We can't go back. Not right now. And there are no humans for miles around us."

"We could go to one of the other cities," Asher suggested, a bit too excited about that unknown prospect. "The other vampires would be happy to take us in, I'm sure."

"And what would we tell them?" The question came out before I could realize I'd said it out loud. Asher shot me a look, but I didn't back down. "Do we tell them the humans kicked us out of our own city? What do you think they will do?" I raised a brow.

"They'll come barging in with fangs out," Maleria answered with a shake of her head. "They won't ask questions. They'll kill whoever is in charge and take the city back, putting us right back to where we started."

I was surprised to see Maleria here. I'd thought she would have been one of the ones to get killed in the attack. It was especially surprising to hear her talk about not wanting to go back to the way things were. It seemed I was wrong about my friend's companion. I'd been wrong about a lot of things.

"She's right." Patrick picked up his own cup and took a drink. "If we let on to what happened in Alban, there will be a massacre even worse than the one the humans created."

"Then what do we do?" Asher said eventually, sagging in his seat. "We just wait here and hope they calm down? That's worse than if they'd just killed us right there."

Patrick sighed. "That's all we can do, for now."

Asher wasn't wrong. Waiting was torture. More vampires showed up at the safe house over the next few days but only a few more. It seemed like the humans had gotten most of them. That didn't bode well for the rest of us.

After a month, Patrick sent Maleria, the quickest and sneakiest of us, to check on the situation. But she only returned with a sad shake of her head. The humans weren't any closer to calming down since the time we left.

"It's a madhouse in there," she told us. "No one seems to know what's going on. One half of the population is still angry, while the other half wants to find a new way to rule Alban. People are stealing and just generally causing destruction."

"It will get better," Asher told her, placing a hand on her shoulder. He and Maleria had come together shortly after our arrival, taking comfort in each other after their losses. I was happy for them, I really was, but I couldn't help but wonder about my own family still in the chaos that had become Alban.

Two more months passed and each month, Patrick sent Maleria to check. Each month she came back with the same sad expression and the same sour news. Until finally, on the fourth month, she came back smiling.

"It's time." She grinned and took hold of Asher's hand. "We can finally go home."

"Are you sure?" Patrick asked, wrapping his arm around me.

"Yes, I'm sure. I even talked to your father." Maleria looked at me. "He wants to meet to discuss terms."

"Ugh." Asher groaned. "More political games."

I beamed up at Patrick, the mention of my father making my heart swell.

We'd gotten closer over the last four months. We still haven't reached that point where we were true husband and wife, but we were getting there. I'd even admitted my feelings for him aloud, which I had been rewarded with a heated kiss that made my toes curl. Each night was a test of my strength because there weren't enough beds to go around, and it only made sense for us to share. I knew eventually that I would give into him, though he never pushed.

I thought I was waiting for this. For this moment, where I didn't have the burden of my family's welfare on my shoulders, and now it had finally happened.

"Are you ready, Clarabelle?" Patrick asked me quietly. I loved the way my name sounded on his lips. It no longer sounded like a name for a cow, but that of someone who was profoundly and irrevocably loved.

Holding him to me tightly, I kissed him and said, "Yes. Let's go play."

About the Author

Erin Bedford is an otaku, recovering coffee addict, and Legend of Zelda fanatic. Her brain is so full of stories that need to be told that she must get them out or explode into a million screaming chibis. Obsessed with fairy tales and bad boys, she hasn't found a story she can't twist to match her deviant mind full of innuendos, snarky humor, and dream guys.

On the outside, she's a work from home mom and bookbinger. One the inside, she's a thirteen-year-old boy screaming to get out and tell you the pervy joke they found online. As an ex-computer programmer, she dreams of one day combining her love for writing and college credits to make the ultimate video game!

Until then, when she's not writing, Erin is devouring as many books as possible on her quest to have the biggest book gut of all time. She's written over thirty books, ranging from paranormal romance, urban fantasy, and even scifi romance.

Come chat me up!
www.erinbedford.com
Facebook.com/erinrbedford
twitter.com/erin_bedford
Don't forget to follow me on Goodreads, Pinterest, Instagram, and YouTube!

Want to be the first to know about my new releases?
Erinbedford.com/newsletter